MW00770748

Orson
Scott
Card

StoneFather

Subterranean Press 2008

First Edition

ISBN 978-1-59606-194-1

Subterranean Press
PO Box 190106
Burton, MI 48519

www.subterraneanpress.com

When Runnel was born, he was given a water name even though there had never been a wetwizard in the family.

In the old days such names were given only to those babies as would be sacrificed to Yeggut, the water god. Later, such names were given to those who would live to serve as priests to Yeggut. Still later, wetnames went to children of families that pretended they once had a watermage in their ancestry.

But now, in the village of Farzibeck, wetnames were given because the mother was fond of a nearby brooklet or because the father had a friend with such a name. This close to Mitherhome, the great city of watermages, it was no surprise that waternames were more popular than any others, even among rude peasants.

Runnel was born to be the rudest of them all, the ninth son and fifteenth child of a farmwife who had the gift of conceiving children readily and bearing them as if her loins were a streambed and each baby a spring flood. Mother had the wide and heavy hips of a woman whose body had reconciled itself to perpetual pregnancy, yet her cheery smile and patient temper still drew men to her more than her husband wished.

Runnel had the misfortune of looking like neither of his parents, so perhaps Father had dark suspicions about the boy's siring. What other explanation could there be for the way Father pointedly ignored him, whenever he wasn't cuffing him or berating him for the constant infraction of being an unloved boy who persisted in existing.

Runnel wasn't especially good at anything, and he wasn't especially bad at anything. He learned the work of a hardscrabble mountain-country farming village as quickly as most, but no quicker; he played the games of children as vigorously as any and enjoyed them as much, but no more. He was too ordinary for anyone to notice him, except that his brothers and sisters could not help but pick up Father's disdain for him, so that he had to fight a bit harder to keep his place when they lined up for food from the stewpot that Mother kept simmering by the fire.

Mother liked him well enough—she liked all her children—but she called them all by each other's names and didn't know enough numbers to take a census and notice when one or two were missing.

Runnel took all these things as his lot in life—he knew nothing else. He flung himself out the door and into whatever day the world presented to him, and came home stinking of sweat from whatever work or play had taken up his hours.

His only distinction, if one could call it that, was that he was a fearless climber of rocks. There was no shortage of cliffs and crags in the vicinity. The children grew up knowing all the grassy paths and steps that allowed them to climb wherever they wanted, with no unusual effort and danger.

But Runnel was impatient with circuitous, gentle routes, and when they all went to play king of the hill or just to look out from one of the lesser crags that overlooked their whole valley, Runnel would go straight up the cliff face, his fingers probing for creases and cracks and ledges and ridges in the stone. He always found them, sooner rather than later—though what was the point, since he rarely reached the pinnacle before anyone else?

His older siblings called him stupid and warned him that they'd refuse to pick up his broken body when it fell. "We'll just leave you for the vultures and the rats to eat." But since he never fell from the cliff, they had no chance to take out their spite on his corpse.

It could have gone on like this forever.

When he reached the age that might have been twelve, if anyone bothered counting, Runnel began to get his man-height, and his face took on the shape it would bear throughout his life. Not that *he* ever saw it—no water in that sloping land held still long enough to see reflections, and he wouldn't have bothered anyway.

Two things happened.

Runnel began to take notice of the village girls, and realized that *they* took no notice of him, though they had eyes for all the other boys of his height. They neither flirted with Runnel nor taunted him. He simply didn't exist to them.

And Father began to be more brutal in his beatings. Perhaps Father thought he finally recognized who Runnel's real sire must have been. Or perhaps he simply recognized that mere cuffings were nothing to Runnel now and it would take more serious effort to explain to him just how despised he was. Whatever the motive, Runnel continued to bear it, though now there were always bruises and sometimes there was blood.

He could bear the disdain of the village girls—many a man had found his bride in another village. He could bear the pain of his father's blows.

What he could not bear and did not understand was the way his brothers and sisters began to avoid him. Father's constant seething rage against him had apparently marked him in their eyes as someone different and shameful. Their father could not be unjust; therefore, Runnel must deserve the mistreatment. The other children did not strike him—it would have been redundant—but they began excluding him from things and playing mean pranks on him.

On a certain day in early spring, when it was still cold, and old snow lay in all northern shadows, the children took it into their minds to run like a flock of geese for the steepest of the crags they were wont to climb, and as Runnel began his own separate ascent, he somehow knew that this was a joke, that when he got to the top he would be all alone, while the others were off somewhere else.

Yet he continued to climb, thinking: I'm too old to play these games, anyway. I should spend my time like the older boys, lounging around or wrestling near the stream, where the girls came to fetch water, and gape and jape and *try* to draw their smiles or, failing that, their disdain or mockery.

But if he tried, then it would shame him and hurt him if they still paid him no attention. Besides, he didn't think any of the village girls were interesting. He didn't care if they noticed him. And he didn't care that when he got to the top of the crag he was all alone.

The world spread out before him. Mountains were all around, but so high was their valley that this crag was merely one among many, and he could see far and wide over the shoulders of the neighboring peaks.

He saw the pass that led over the Mitherkame—for in Farzibeck they had other names for the other mountains, and only used the sacred name for the great spine of mountains that lined up in a long row like the ragged teeth of a fighting sword—sharp obsidian flakes jutting from between the two halves of a split branch.

The track that crossed it between two of its sharp teeth was called "the Utteroad" if you went west toward Uhetter, and "the Mitheroad" if you went east. That path, the travelers said, would take you down to the great valley of Mitherhome, the city of the water wizards, which was surrounded on all sides by holy water.

On the pass, Runnel could see a wagon moving up the grassy road, though it was so far off that he only knew it to be a wagon because of how slowly and lurchingly it moved. And maybe he could see the animal pulling it, or maybe it was just a blur in the cold sunlight.

He thought, Why am I here, when I could be there?

And with no more contemplation than that, he climbed down the crag on the side toward the Mitheroad, and did not even pass through the village, still less come near the family farm, on his way through the meadows and fields and woods. He came to the Mitheroad just as it began its last ascent over the Mitherkame, and ran easily up the grassy path.

Only when he stood at the very spot where he had seen the wagon did he stop and look back toward Farzibeck. Runnel had never been to this place before, and had never looked at his village from so far away. It took him a considerable time even to find it. As for his family's farm, it was just a brown lump of a hovel in the midst of a meadow. In a week or so, Father would start to break up the earth with his son-drawn plow, and then the meadow would disappear, and bare earth would take its place. But right now, the farm looked no different from countless meadows and clearings. It was as if all their work there amounted to nothing.

I'm hungry, thought Runnel, and he turned away from the vista to search for wild onion and crumbleroot. It was standard spring fare, to help eke out what was left of the winter stores, but of course the travelers now moving along the road would have taken much if not all of the scavengeable food.

Yet he found plenty to eat, as soon as he started to look, and wondered if this was because crumble and onion grew so thick that it outgrew the travelers' taking, or because the travelers were laboring so hard to get up and over the pass that they did not think of food when they came to the crest.

Or maybe they disdained the biting onion and the bitter crumble. Many did. Mother would add them to the stew in spring, and even though Runnel thought they added a delicious tang, some of his brothers complained that they poisoned the whole thing and made them want to vomit. They never *did* vomit, however, and Mother got them to eat without complaint by saying that crumble was medicinal and would make better swordsmen of them. How they laughed at Runnel, when he was little, for asking when they would start practicing with their swords, now that they had eaten the stew with crumble in it.

Runnel dug up five good-sized crumble roots and a dozen small onions, used grass to wipe off the dirt as best he could, and then made a basket of his shirtfront in order to hold them. Tying the shirt closed brought it well above his waist, so his middle got cold in the nippy air, even though it was high noon. But better to be cold than hungry, for vigorous walking would make him warmer *and* hungrier by day's end. He'd feel foolish, perhaps, if nightfall brought him to a place with plenty of food to scavenge; but better to carry food he didn't need than to be without it in some lonely stretch of unfamiliar wood, where he would not know which berries and mushrooms were safe to eat, and so have to spend the night with nothing in his belly.

The other side of the pass showed him a world not much different from the side he lived on, except that the peaks in front of him were lower than those behind. As the day wore on, and he walked down one slope and up another, the peaks ceased to be snow-covered. Finally the road stopped being a track in the thick grass of an endless meadow and became a wide, flat, and gravelly ledge cut from the hills by the labor of men, flanking a stream deep and swift enough that it might have been a river, had there been room enough for one in the narrow valley. The water tumbled around boulders and roared over short but savage falls, so Runnel stayed well clear of the road's edge, for he had no fear of falling from rock, but this water had power that he did not understand.

No wonder the great mages drew their power from water. It was mighty in a way that the mountains could never be. For the water might be smaller, but it was vigorous, while the mountains always seemed to be resting or even asleep. What good was it to be a giant if you never stirred, while small waters raced across your body, cutting canyons in your stony flesh?

And yet it was the mountains that he loved, the roughness and hardness of their bones where they protruded from the soil, and it was the water that he feared. How silly to fear the thing for which you were named, he told himself. I wish they had named me Cobble or Pebble or Rock or Boulder or Crag or Ledge or any other word referring to stone. Then perhaps

Father would never have beaten me, for what man would dare to strike stone?

He came to a place where the road veered away from the river and went up and over a hill. But he could hear a roaring sound and had to see, so he left the road and climbed the rocks high above the river until he came to a place where the rock simply stopped.

It was like the edge of one world and the beginning of another. Here he was, as he had always been, in the hard high stoneland of the Mitherkame; there, far below, was a land of soft greens and rolling hills, surrounding the Mitherlough, a huge lake that, for all Runnel knew, could have been the great Sea itself, where Skruplek the Sailor had all the adventures that were told about on winter evenings when the short days left them in darkness long before they were sleepy.

The river flew out from the clifftop and fell into mist that clung like a shy cloud to the cliff's face. Beyond, the great expanse of fields was dotted with houses, all of them obviously larger than his family's hovel; and the villages were far more populous than the few wooden houses of Farzibeck.

Only after he had been looking for some few minutes did he realize that the rocky mount at the right-hand side of the lake was lined with stone and wooden buildings, right to the crest, and high stone walls rose above the treetops in the wild forest that stretched between him and the Mitherlough. It was the city of Mitherhome.

He could see now where the road he had been following emerged from the mountains, far to the right of where he stood, winding its way around the forest and down below the lake, as if it meant to miss the city entirely. That was no good to him. Maybe it joined a road that came back up to the city and

maybe it didn't. But he wouldn't take the chance. It was the city he wanted, and to the city he would go, road or no road.

He swung himself over the cliff edge and began climbing down. It was always harder to descend an unfamiliar cliff; his feet had to find gaps and cracks and ledges that his eyes had never seen. But he did all right, and it took him far less time to get to the bottom of the cliff than it would have taken him to follow the road.

The trouble was that no one else ever used this route, so there was not so much as a path. Which was particularly annoying because the waterfall made so thick a fog at the bottom that he could not see more than a step ahead. But he found a place where a finger of stone spread from the cliff like the root from a tree, and where the stone grew, the trees couldn't, so he made his way easily for some time.

By the time the last of the stone finger plunged under the soil, the air was clear again and he could see. Not that the trees left him much view, they were so thick; but now he could find deer paths and, as long as he kept within earshot of the tumbling river to his left, he knew he would not lose his way.

Still, it was slow going, and the sun was getting low—no more than two palms above the horizon, he estimated—when he came to the stone wall he had seen from the top of the cliff.

Now he saw that the wall was in ruins. He had thought the wall rose and fell with the terrain, but instead the land was fairly level, and the stone wall had simply collapsed—or been torn down. There was nowhere near enough stone to account for the gaps in the wall. He could only conclude that people had come here and carted away the huge cut stones that were once part of the wall.

The sky was red with sunset when he came to the end of his path. For instead of leading him up to the mount where the city perched, as it had seemed from the cliff top, the river took him to an arm of the lake. Across the water he could see there were torchlights in the city and along what had to be stone bridges spanning the gaps through which water poured from the larger lake beyond into this smaller one.

There was no bridge across *this* river, though. And Runnel, having never seen so much water, also had no notion of swimming; he knew the word only as something fish and geese did. The water of Farzibeck was too cold, shallow, and swift for anything but a barefoot splash in summer; the rest of the time, they used staves to leap the few streams too wide to step over.

Knowing he could not go north, he walked south along the edge of the lake and came to a stone tower. This was not in ruins—indeed, it was surrounded by a goat-trimmed meadow, and the wide stone steps that led from the tower, down to the lake were swept clean. Yet no light shone from the tower and when Runnel thought of calling out to hail anyone who might be inside, it occurred to him that he did not know this place, and perhaps the reason that there were no paths in this wood was that the place was forbidden. For now he saw that this tower was a giant version of the small altars that were erected beside every stream in the vicinity of Farzibeck. What else could he have expected? Such large waters cried out for giant altars—for stone towers like this one.

He realized it was a tower of living stone, all of one piece, as if it had been carved from a natural crag that once stood here—it had not been stacked up from pebbles or cobbles like most little altars.

Runnel moved on along the lakeshore until he came to a place where the lake poured out onto a tumble of stone and down into a steep-walled canyon. There was no crossing here, either. No wonder the huge stone wall behind him had been left to fall in ruins. What need had Mitherhome of a city wall on this side? No enemy could cross this barrier.

Yet on the other side of the rapids more walls stood, even higher than the ones he had passed before, though also with ruined gaps, and undefended. Once this city had felt the need of walls despite the water barrier that protected them. Now, though, they did not, or the walls would not be left in disrepair.

Well, it hardly mattered how permeable the walls beyond this canyon were, for he could not cross it. There was nowhere to go except along its edge to see if it was bridged somewhere.

As soon as he thought of bridges, he saw that it had once been bridged right here. Runnel could still see, in the waning light, the nubs of the bridge that had once spanned the chasm. As best he could tell, the bridge had been like the tower—all of a piece, not made of piled stone or wood. Yet it had broken somehow, and fallen, and Runnel could imagine that some of the boulders over which the water tumbled in the rapids below had once been part of the bridge.

It was growing dark. And though it was warmer here in the wide valley of Mitherhome than it had been up in the high mountains, it was still chilly and would get colder through the night.

And for the first time all day, Runnel thought: What am I doing here? Why have I come? What do I want? I could have been home, warm in the pile of brothers and sisters on the straw floor of our hovel. Not stuck between two rivers and a lake, in an abandoned forest, in sight of ruined walls, with a great city out of reach.

Even if I get to the city, I have no friends or kin there. No one will owe me a meal or a place by the fire.

Tomorrow I'll go back through the forest and climb up the cliff and follow the road home.

Then he thought of his father beating him for having stayed out a whole night, and for coming home weary and empty-handed. "What are you good for?" his father would ask.

"Nothing," Runnel would answer. And it would be true.

The story of his useless journey would quickly spread, and the girls who already ignored him would despise him. He would have even less honor than the none he already had.

He could be friendless and cold here as well as anywhere. And tomorrow I'll find a way into the city.

He untied his shirt and methodically chewed and swallowed the crumbleroot, adding a bite of onion now and then to take away the bitterness. It was not good food, especially because his own body heat and sweat had made it all just a little soggy. But it filled him. He thought of saving some for tomorrow, but he knew the insects would have it before dawn, and he needed his shirt for warmth. He could go a day or two without food if he had to. He'd done it before, in a long winter, when the older children ate nothing at some meals so the little ones wouldn't go without. And other times, when he could not face a cuffing from his father, Runnel would skip his supper and ask for no food when he came in late. Nor, on those occasions, had there been some favorite brother or sister who saved him something.

He hollowed a place for himself among the cold damp fallen leaves near the cliff edge, so he lay on stone, and gathered more leaves to pull on top of himself where he curled on the ground. Others sought soil to sleep on, when they were caught out of doors, but to Runnel, the stone might be cold, but it wasn't damp, and it never left him sore and filthy the way soil did.

At this lower elevation it did not get as cold at night. He slept warmly enough that during the night he cast off some of the leaves that covered him.

In the morning he had nothing to eat, and he could hear few birds through the din of the rapids just over the edge of the cliff. But he had slept well and arose invigorated, and today he did not even think of turning back. Instead he went to the right, mostly southward, skirting the edge of the cliff. The water tumbled farther and farther below, so that even though the ground he walked on sloped downward, it was ever higher above the water.

He came to a wall, which he recognized as a continuation of the ruined wall he had passed through yesterday. Only this wall was not in ruins, and he could hear conversation; it was manned, and though the guards were careless enough to let their chatter be heard, the fact that anyone was keeping vigil meant that there must be something ahead of him that needed guarding.

There was no door or break in the wall here, so there was no point in hailing the guards. Instead, Runnel walked along the woods well back from the wall, looking for a gate.

It was a huge thing, when he reached it, and it was held shut by huge bars. It baffled him: The bars were on his side of the gate. He was *inside* whatever it was protecting. In the middle of the gate was a small door, which a man would have to stoop to get through. But it had the great virtue of being open.

Runnel headed for it. Almost at once he was seized by the shoulder and roughly tripped.

"Where do you think you're going, fool?" said a soft voice.

Runnel rolled over and saw a man standing over him, holding a javelin. Not a soldier, though, for the javelin was his only weapon, and he wore only simple cloth. A hunter? "Through the gate," said Runnel. Where else would he be going?

"And have your throat slit and all your blood drained into the river?" asked the hunter.

Runnel was baffled. "Who would do such a thing to a mere traveler?"

"No one," said the hunter. "It would be done to a fool of a boy who wandered through the sacred forest, thus declaring himself to be a sacrifice, and a right worthy one, in the eyes of them as still think that water needs blood from time to time."

"How would *I* know it was sacred?" asked Runnel.

"Didn't you feel the bones of the dead among the trees? The soldiers who fell here to the bronze swords of Veryllydd still whisper to *me*—I don't forget the blood that made this place holy. But the beasts I hunt for the sacrifice are like you—they don't know it's a sacred wood. They're going about their business when I snare them or pierce them."

"Are you going to kill me, then?"

"I was asked for two hares, and so I'll find hares and bring them. If they asked for a stupid peasant boy from the mountains, *then* I'd truss you up and drag you in."

"All I want is —"

"All you want is to be another useless adventurous lad from the mountains who'll make himself a nuisance to everyone in the city until you give up and go back home where you belong. There's nothing for you here."

"Then I *am* home," said Runnel defiantly, "for home has always been a place with nothing for me."

The hunter smiled a little. "A sharp wit. With that mouth, and that proud look on your face, you'll probably get beaten to death before you starve."

Proud look? How could he look proud, lying on his back in the dirt and old leaves? "Either way," said Runnel, "I'd like to spend some of the brief time I have left inside the city of Mitherhome, but all I find is broken walls and broken bridges and rivers I can't cross."

The man sighed. "Here's what you do if you're determined to suffer more before you go home. There's another gate farther along. *Don't* go near it. Nor should you go near the four houses that are just inside the gate. Skirt wide around them and go on in sight of the wall till you come to a place where the wall is broken down. Go through the gap, then head straight south till you come to the Uhetter Road. Try to act like you just left the road to take a piss and you've been traveling on it all day, instead of traipsing through the holy wood."

"Will the road take me in to Mitherhome?" asked Runnel.

"The road will just sit there," said the hunter. "Your legs will take you to Hetterferry, and from there maybe you will and maybe you won't figure out a way to get onto the ferry boat and into Low Mitherhome without your miserable country bumpkin rags getting too wet."

Runnel was curious. "Why are you helping me?"

"I'm not helping you. I'm getting rid of you."

"But I've stepped in the sacred wood."

"I live in it. If the spirits of the sacred dead minded your passage, they would have tripped you with their bones or terrified you with their whispers, and they chose not to. Who am *I* to complain of you?"

"So you serve Yeggut, the water god, and yet you allow me to live?"

"There *is* no water god," said the hunter kindly. "I'm employed by the priests who put on the sacrifices to please the ignorant people who *think* there's a water god. Anyone with even a scrap of sense knows that the watermages do their work, not by praying to some god, but by speaking directly to the water itself."

"So...doesn't that make the water a god?"

"It makes the water *water,* and the mages *mages,*" said the hunter. "Now go away. And don't even think of asking me for food, or I'll pierce you after all and let them pour you out to give Holy Yeggut a drink."

His mention of "drink" made Runnel thirsty, but he made no request and walked, then ran, deeper into the wood, away from the wall.

He worked his way west, and stayed far enough away from the next gate that he saw neither it nor the houses the hunter had described. Not much farther, he came to the ruined wall, and followed it till he found a gap. Then he went back toward the south, and found yet another gap, which must have been the one the hunter meant, but it made no difference except a few extra steps. Then he reached the corner of the wall where it turned eastward, and here again was a well-maintained tower with guards in it, looking out over the wood. How stupid, thought Runnel, to have a wall that you can simply walk around, and yet defend one short section of it. Are your foes so lazy you can let most of your wall fall down and they won't even bother to walk through it?

Soon he reached the road. There was no one in sight. He stepped out and walked east along the shores of a different stream. This one was shallower and broader—it looked like it could be forded. And sure enough, he soon came to a place where wagons on another road from the south crossed the river and joined the Uhetter Road.

No one hailed him, though as he neared the wagons he got some suspicious glances. Not wishing trouble, Runnel skirted them widely and ran on ahead, to make it obvious he wasn't there to steal or beg or whatever it was they feared he'd try. I've errands of my own.

Soon the road ran between houses and shops. From some of the houses came the smell of food, and when Runnel saw that people were going freely in and out of one of them, he concluded it was a roadhouse and he went inside.

He was stopped at once by a burly man who said, "Have you got money, boy?"

Runnel looked around, confused. "What's a money?" he asked.

The man laughed nastily and shoved him out. "What's a money!" he said. "They come stupider and more arrogant about it every spring!"

So getting a meal would be harder than Runnel had thought. In Farzibeck, any home would open its door to a traveler, and ask no more of him than news or whatever gift he chose to give. Who ever heard of a roadhouse demanding a particular gift—especially one that Runnel had never heard of! How could he have brought a "money" when he didn't know what it was and had no idea where to find one and couldn't have guessed in advance that they'd even *want* such a thing?

Madness. But from the way other people in the roadhouse laughed at him, he could only conclude that everybody here knew what moneys were, and knew the innkeeper would demand it of them. So it was a city thing, and he would have to find out about it. But not here.

Not far into the town of Hetterferry, he came to a dock on what looked to be another lake, though not as large as the Mitherlough. He soon realized, from the conversations he overheard, that this was the river called Ronnyrill, which flowed down in three streams from the lake high above, then on to Ronys and Abervery and other strange, exotic-sounding places. Much good that would do him, though. What mattered to him was that the real city of Mitherhome was plainly visible, not more than a stone's throw away at the nearest point, but the torrent of water pouring out of the deep gash in the cliff made a more impassible barrier than their ridiculous wall.

When he asked a man about the ferry boat, he once again heard the word "money."

"Does everyone here demand the same gift in trade?"

In reply, the man smiled and reached into a pouch tucked into the sash that bound his shirt closed. He pulled out a single half-blackened disc of bronze. "Money," he said. "You get it by working, and then you trade it for things you want."

"But it's so small," said Runnel.

"So's your wit," said the man, and turned away.

At least now he knew how to get money—you worked. That was something Runnel knew how to do. He walked along the dock till he came to a boat that was busy with men carrying crates onto a large raft. A man was standing by a crate, apparently waiting for one of the other laborers to come and carry the other end with him. So Runnel squatted and put his hands under the crate and said, "Let's do it."

The laborer looked at him, shrugged, and took up his end. Together they carried it onto the raft, which seemed to Runnel to be as big as his whole village. Runnel stayed with the job for half an hour, working as hard as any of the adult men. But when it was done, everybody else got on the raft and pushed off, leaving him behind. He wanted to cry out to them that all he wanted was to cross the stupid river, what would that cost them? But he knew that they knew what he wanted, and they had chosen to take his labor and pay him nothing, and there was nothing he could do about it. Begging wouldn't change their minds—it would only invite their scorn. Besides, the men he had helped were hirelings themselves—they were not the men who could have rewarded him with passage. Runnel had been a fool.

He was very, very hungry now—and thirsty, too. The water of the river didn't look terribly clean, despite having just come out of the canyon. From the look of it, all the waste of the city was dumped into the Mitherlough above and got carried down in the torrent. So he would need water to replace what he had sweated out.

Back home, if you needed a drink, you knelt by a brook or runnel somewhere and drank your fill. It was all clean—there was no village upstream of them. And they left it clean—it was a matter of piety not to dishonor Yeggut by polluting the streams that flowed near them. But they had heard from travelers that the sewers of the great cities flowed right out into the water, as if the god were nothing to them. Now, having heard what the hunter in the sacred wood said of the god, Runnel believed the tale.

That meant he needed to find water from upstream of this town. It would mean leaving again, and it occurred to him that once he set foot on the Uhetter Road he would probably let it carry him all the way back to Farzibeck.

He took a different street away from the dock, and almost immediately found himself at a public fountain, with water gushing from the mouths of three stone fish into three pools into which women were dipping jars and pails to carry back to houses and shops.

Grateful for the bounty, Runnel dropped to his knees beside one of the pools and splashed water up into his face.

Almost immediately, he was once again seized by the shoulder, and once again he was hurled down, though this time he sprawled, not on dirt and leaves, but on the hard cobblestones of the street. A large woman loomed over him, her jar standing on the ground beside her.

"What do you mean, putting your filthy hands right in the water! And then washing the dust from your own face right back into it for the rest of us to drink!"

"I'm sorry," said Runnel. "But don't you dip your jar in? And isn't it standing on the ground right now, getting filthy?"

"But it's my jar," she said, "and I only set it down to drag your filthy head out of the fountain."

"I didn't put my head in," said Runnel.

"Might as well have! Now get away before I call the guard on you!"

"I'm thirsty," said Runnel. "Where else can I get water?"

"Back in your hometown!" she roared. "Or pee into your hand and drink *that!*" Then she picked up her jar, made a great show of brushing off the bottom of it, and dipped it into the fountain, her huge buttocks pointed directly at Runnel.

The stones had bruised him about as well as Father ever did. Runnel knew how to move carefully and slowly until he knew exactly where it hurt most, so he'd know how to get up with the minimum of pain.

"Are you all right?" asked a young woman.

"You mean apart from being thirsty, hungry, embarrassed, and bruised?"

"All right, then, *be* proud," she retorted, and carried her jar to the fountain.

"What did I say?" asked Runnel. "You asked how I was, and I'm thirsty, hungry, embarrassed, and bruised. It was an honest answer."

"And still you have that proud look about you," she said, after a mere glance. "I see you think you're better than anyone."

"I know that I'm not," said Runnel. "And if there's a proud look on my face, Yeggut put it there, not me." For the first time, Runnel wondered if there was something wrong with his face, and that was why his father hated him.

The girl's jar was full. She rocked it up so it stood in the fountain, then turned and faced him, her hands on her hips. She was a girl who worked hard, for her bare arms were muscled and her face was brown. But she was also clean and so was her clothing. He had never seen a girl in clothes so clean. She must wear it no more than a week without washing.

"You're not mocking me?" asked the girl.

"Why would I mock you?" said Runnel. "You were kindly to me, asking how I was, which makes you the best person I've met so far in this place."

"You say fair enough words," she said, "but your face and your voice and your manner still look disdainful. The god *was* unkind to you. That face should have belonged to a lord or a mage—then no one would mind the proud look."

"No one in my village ever told me," said Runnel. "They must be used to me, having seen this face since I was a baby."

"Oh, and you think you're *not* a baby now?" she said, with a bit of smile at the corners of her mouth.

"Now who's the mocker?" asked Runnel.

"That's different," she said. "You really *are* small."

"I can't help being young. I'm growing, though—I'm taller than I was. I can work hard. I do what I'm told. I can't help my face, but I can bow my head and hide it—see?"

He tucked his chin onto his chest.

"Couldn't get much work done in that position," she said. "But no use asking me for work, I haven't any such thing in my gift. I'm a servant myself, though *not* a slave, thank the god, so

I get a coin now and then, and the master couldn't make free with me even if he wanted to, which he's too old even to wish for, thank the god."

"Then let me carry your waterjar for you, and you can let me ask your master for work."

"It's a great household, lad," she said. "You wouldn't speak to the master, you'd speak to Demwor, the steward."

"The what?"

"The man who rules the servants, under my master. The man who keeps the counts. The guardian, the—you've *never* heard the word 'steward'?"

"There's not more than three servants in my whole village, and no house with two of them." Runnel thought of each of them, all of them old, and belonging to houses once headed by men who went off to the wars and came home rich. They had been captured by the men's own hand as spoils of war, which made them slaves by the decision of the gods. Now the men were long dead, and the servants were old, and hardly anybody cared that they weren't free. The only reason Runnel knew was that when he was little, he asked why one of them had never married, and then the whole business of servants was explained to him, and the other two were pointed out as well.

And here he was, volunteering to be a servant himself. Only, like this girl, he intended to be one who was free, and made a—what was the word? A coin now and then.

"If you drop the jar, I'll be beaten for it, free or not," she said. "And no payment for you—I have no coin to spare. Nor kisses neither, in case you thought."

"What?" he asked, dumfounded.

"In *case*," she said. "You claimed not to be a baby any more."

"I wouldn't just...why would I?"

She narrowed her eyes. "And here I thought you weren't really proud," she said.

"I didn't mean..." And then he gave up and hefted the jar out of the water. It was heavy. They never used such large jugs in Farzibeck, but that was partly because water was never very far away, and none of the houses used much water, and who could afford a jar *this* big?

He hugged it to his belly and she eyed him critically. "Get a hand more under it in front...yes...no, lower, catch under the edge like...like that. You don't want it sliding through your arms to land on your feet."

"Maybe I should balance it on my head," said Runnel.

"You might carry a basket of feathers that way," she said, "but you don't have enough of a neck to balance water there. First your neck would break, and then the jar."

"Can we start moving?" he said. "Because I can't hold this forever."

The nasty woman who had shoved and threatened him had apparently stayed to gossip with other women. Now she saw Runnel carrying the jar and she called out to the servant girl, "Ho, Lark, don't you know that fine lordling will take what he wants from you and run away?"

"They only run away from *you*, Wesera!" Lark cheerfully called back.

"Don't know how she thinks I could run anywhere, carrying this," muttered Runnel.

Lark burst out laughing. "You really *are* fresh from the farm, aren't you!"

"Why? What did I say?"

"No, no, I think it's sweet that you don't think that way. You really *don't*, do you? And not because you're too young, either. Now you know my name's Lark, so what's *your* name, since it seems I'm about to introduce you to Demwor and I ought to know it."

"Runnel."

"Is that because you peed yourself all the time as a baby?" she said. "Or is there water magic in your family?"

"I didn't choose my name," said Runnel, embarrassed and a little angry. "No one mocked me for it where I lived."

"I'm not mocking you!" said Lark. "I've just never—it's the kind of name a man takes when he's joining the service of Yeggut. The kind of name watermages give their children."

"Half the children in Farzibeck have water names," said Runnel. "It shows that your parents are waterfolk."

"It's a good name. It's just that in Mitherhome they go more for ancient names or trade names or virtues. I'm not from here, either—my family farms to the east of here, and northward. I was named for a meadowbird that my mother loves to hear singing. So you can be named for a brook, and it's no shame. I was just surprised."

"Then let's agree never to mock each other," said Runnel, "so that even if it sounds like it, or looks like it, we'll both know that no harm is meant."

"*If* Demwor hires you, which is unlikely, and *if* we have occasion to see each other again—also unlikely—then yes, I agree, I won't mock you."

"Thank you."

"To your face, anyway," she said. Only she was grinning in a way that said that indeed no harm was intended.

I'm going to hide my face from everybody, thought Runnel. *And* my name. People find the one offensive and the other ridiculous. And I had to come all these miles to find out about it.

They walked in silence for a little while. Then Runnel could not contain it. "What's *wrong* with my face."

"Nothing," she said. "You're not handsome, you're not ugly."

"What makes you say I look proud?"

"Well it's the whole thing. The expression."

"What about the expression?"

"I don't know," she said, sounding exasperated. "You just do. Like you're a statue."

"What's a statue?"

"How can I explain it if you—a statue is made of stone or metal or clay, and it shows a person's face, only it doesn't move, it just stays exactly the same."

"I move my face. I talk. I smile. I move my eyes. I nod my head."

"Well stop doing it or you'll drop the jar."

"Did you have to fill it completely full?"

"Do you want me to carry it now?"

He would not have a girl carry something because he could not. "I can do it."

"You want to know what's wrong with your face? I'll tell you. Right now you were annoyed with me—for filling it so full, and then for offering to carry it. But *nothing* showed in your face. You moved your mouth, you moved your eyes, but you didn't show anything you were thinking. It looks like you think you're better than me. Like you don't have to bother feeling anything about me."

"Well I *was* annoyed. I can't help what my face shows."

"And you're annoyed now, and it *still* doesn't show."

Runnel made a monstrous face. "How about now?"

"Now you're ugly. But it still doesn't look like you mean it."

It was a shocking thing to learn about himself. "Why didn't anybody ever tell me?"

"Probably because they thought you were proud and didn't like them, so why should they tell you anything?"

"So why are *you* telling me?"

"Because I saw you knocked in the dirt by Wesera and you looked thirsty and miserable. Your *face* looked proud, so I thought that meant you had spunk. Now you say you aren't proud, so that must mean you *don't* have spunk, so…no, we said no mockery, so…I believe you. I believe you can't help it. But you know what helps? Ducking your head. Makes you look humble. Hides the stiffness. Do that a lot, and people won't want to slap you around."

"Do *you* want to slap me around?"

"Two answers to that. No, because you're carrying my water for me. And no, because I don't care enough to slap you, and I'm never going to, so if that was your first test to see if you could get close to me —"

He was sick of her assumption that he had some interest in her like that. So he walked faster and moved briskly ahead of her.

"Watch out, slow down!" she shouted. "You'll drop it, you'll break it, you'll spill it!"

Water *was* sloshing and splashing, so he did as she asked and she was beside him again.

"So you don't like me," she said. "I get it."

"I like you fine," he said. "You helped me. I just don't want anything from you except a chance at a job so I can get some of these moneys or coins or whatever you call them. And maybe, just maybe, a drink of this water after we get it to wherever we're going."

"Well, that would be now, because we're here." She led him to a doorway in a large, high stone wall.

She stopped outside the door and whistled—a bit of birdsong, it sounded like. She grinned at him and said, "Lark."

The door swung open, and for a moment Runnel thought it was magic. But no, there was a tall stupid-looking man pushing it outward, and Lark flounced through saucily. "Let my boy in, will you?" she said to the man.

Runnel flashed with anger for a moment, but then realized that she was just playing, and besides, just now his only hope of a drink and a meal *was* her. At least she was letting him in. She could have said, Take the water jar and get rid of this boy, and he could have done no more about it than with the men on the cargo raft. He was inside. That was a good thing. So he said nothing, just followed her through the door and into the courtyard.

She led him to a stone structure about the height of a man and half more, with stone stairs winding around two sides of it. She motioned for him to climb the stairs behind her, and when he got to the top, she had already opened a small trapdoor in the roof of the thing. "Pour it in."

He did.

She took the empty jar from him. "I'll carry it now."

"Now it's empty," he said.

"Believe it or not, *this* is the time when people are most likely to break the jar. Once it's empty, it feels light, and you get careless. Only I'd be the one in trouble, not you. So I carry it down. Now move on down out of my way, Runnel, or I'll mock you."

"Then you'd be an oathbreaker."

"Your back will be to me, so I can mock you without breaking the oath."

"Mock me all you want, I don't care."

He shambled down the steps and headed for the door in the garden wall. The tall stupid-looking man was still standing there.

"Wait," she said. "Are you really angry?"

"I'm not angry, I just need to get a drink of water and a bite of food and a job, and it's obvious it's not going to happen here."

"Why, because I teased you?"

"Because you teased me after you promised not to," said Runnel. "You don't keep your word."

She grabbed his shirt and pulled him back. She was *strong*.

She got right in his face. "That was not mocking. That was friendship. Haven't you ever had a friend?"

He almost made a sharp retort, but then he realized: Probably not.

"Mocking you is when I make fun of you in front of people you care about, so it shames you. And I'll never do that, because I took an oath, and because I don't do that to people anyway. How did you get to be this old without knowing anything about people? Were you raised in a cave?"

No, I was raised in my father's house.

She tugged again on his shirt and he followed her to the other side of the cistern where he had just poured the water.

Down low, so she had to stoop, there was an opening, into which she set one of several beakers that stood on a table nearby. She placed it carefully in the middle of a circle etched in the stone base of the opening, and then pressed on a block of stone beside it. Immediately water started trickling into the beaker. It was steady, and the beaker filled faster than Runnel would have expected from the amount of flow.

She let up on the stone she had pressed, and the flow stopped almost at once. She handed the beaker to Runnel.

Runnel took it solemnly. It was a giving of water, and so he murmured the prayer of thanks and then offered it back to her.

"Oh, I forgot, you come from a pious village," she said. "Look, this doesn't mean we're married or anything, does it?"

"It means I'm grateful for the water." Then Runnel brought it to his mouth and began to sip, letting it fill and clean his mouth before swallowing, making sure not to let a drop spill, not even to dribble down his cheeks. The feeling of slakethirst was so strong it took a while for him even to notice the flavor of the water.

"It tastes like a mountain spring, straight from the rock," he said. "It tastes clean."

"Of course," she said. "The water we pour in above seeps through stone, just like a mountain spring."

"I never heard of the watermages needing stone to purify their water."

"Of course not," said Lark. "But my master won't let them purify his water. He insists that he'll draw his water from the same fountain as anyone, and filter it himself, without water-magic touching it."

"Why?" asked Runnel.

"Oh, you don't know, do you," she said. "My master is Brickel. The stonemage of Mitherhome." She said it as if Runnel should know all about it.

But the only thing Runnel knew was that there *were* no stonemages in Mitherhome. He said so.

"It's true there are none *in* Mitherhome," said Lark. "You can see we're in Hetterferry, across flowing water from Low Mitherhome. But he's still the stonemage *of* Mitherhome.

The one they allow to live nearby, in exchange for keeping their walls and bridges and temples in good repair. Keeping the stone from cracking and crumbling, repairing the damage from ice and snow in winter. Even the watermages of Mitherhome need stonework, and that means a stonemage, if you want things made of stone to last, in the presence of so much water."

"You serve a mage?" he said. "Then why aren't *you* proud?"

"Because," she said, lowering her voice, "he's a *stone*mage. They need him here, but they keep constant watch, lest he start trying to bring other stonemages here. Because they need one stonemage to keep their city in repair, but too many stonemages could bring the whole thing toppling down and break open the sacred Mitherlough."

"Why would stonemages do that?"

"Maybe they have cause," said Lark. "All I know is, people don't get in my way because they know whose servant I am, and that he's a powerful man, and no one dares offend him. But nobody wants to befriend him, either. So...nor have I any particular friends in Hetterferry."

"Except among the servants here."

She rolled her eyes. "Oh, yes, we're one big happy family."

"So why do you work here?"

"Because I was an ignorant farm girl when I came here and could find no work. And Master Brickel could find no servants worth anything. I knew nothing, but I worked hard and learned fast. I get coin and I save some and send some home to my family. My brothers are paying a teacher to learn them their letters, from the money I send. So you see? I'm a servant here, and they can hire a servant *there*, and my brothers will have a chance to be clerks, maybe."

"And what will you have a chance to be?"

She looked at him like he was insane. "A servant in a mage's house. You think I don't know how lucky I am to be here?"

The only question in Runnel's mind was: Will *I* be as lucky?

Silently he finished drinking, watching her closely. Watching her face, how she cocked her head to watch him drink, how there were tiny changes in her face reflecting whatever thought she was thinking. He realized that he had always been able to judge other people's moods by what their face showed. It had never occurred to him that nobody could judge *his*.

He thought of the stupid man at the doorway. How did Runnel know the man was stupid? Because of the slack-looking face, the way his grin seemed to have no purpose in it. From his size, he might have been set at the door to guard it. But from the apparent lack of wit, he was there just to open and close it, this being the full extent of his skills.

What if he wasn't stupid? What if his face simply was slack, and he was actually quite keen-witted?

The stupid man's face showed him a lackwit; Runnel's own face showed him proud and aloof. Lark's face showed her to be friendly, quickwitted, but also earnest.

"So when you look at me like that," she said, "what are you thinking?"

"I'm thinking that I wish I knew how to make my face as clever and generous as yours."

She blushed. "I would slap a *man* if he said such a thing to me," she said.

"Why?" he asked, genuinely puzzled.

"Because when a man says such things to a woman, he wants something from her."

"I don't," he said. He held up the half-empty beaker. "Already got what I wanted."

He felt a hand on his shoulder and immediately began to drop toward the ground, so when this person shoved him down he wouldn't fall so far.

But the hand didn't shove him, and Lark greeted the owner of it with a smile. "Demwor," she said, "I want you to meet this lad. His name is Runnel, he's from the mountain village of Farzibeck, he carried a full jar for me the whole way without spilling any, and he doesn't want to get under my skirt."

"Yet," said a soft, deep voice. Runnel tried to turn to see the face from which it came, and found that the hand held him fast.

"He's a different sort," she said. "I think he might be worth it."

"I think he must be a fool," said Demwor, "to let you talk him into carrying a *full* jar."

Only now did Runnel realize that she must have meant to spill out some of the water before carrying it herself. He glared at her, and then realized that perhaps it didn't look like a glare. Perhaps none of the looks he gave people meant anything. What if he always looked the same.

But she smiled benignly at him. "I didn't know you then," she said. "And besides, you *were* strong enough to carry it full, because you did."

"Who told you we were looking to hire someone?" asked Demwor.

"What, are we?" asked Lark.

"No," said Demwor.

"Then it's a good thing I didn't promise him anything except a drink of water and an introduction to you."

So that was it. Another trick. Only now he had water in him, so it wasn't as bad as the first one. Except he was even wearier now, and still had to go out and find a meal and a job.

"You don't like him?" asked Demwor.

"Of course I like him," she said. "Do you think I'd bring somebody I hated? What if you *did* hire him?"

"What I'm asking," said Demwor, "is whether the two of you are going to make a baby here at Lord Brickel's expense."

Lark looked at Runnel with a cocky smile. "I *told* you that's what men always think of."

"Sir," said Runnel, "I work hard, and I learn as fast as anyone, and I keep my word."

"Whom did you run away from?"

"Nobody that will miss me," said Runnel.

The hand tightened on his shoulder. "The name of your master."

"No master, sir," said Runnel. "My father and mother. But I'm the ninth son. As I said, I'll not be missed."

"No mother will come weeping at the gate, complaining we kidnapped her little boy?"

"No one will *notice* I'm gone, sir." Except Father, Runnel thought. He won't have anyone to beat. Still, there was no point in saying *that.* If he mentioned that he had ever been beaten, Demwor would think it was for good reason and assume he was a troublemaker.

"So why did you come here?"

"Because where else does a ninth son go?" he asked. And realized, finally, that it was true. No one had ever explained it to him, but that, as much as his proud face, was why none of the village girls ever looked at him. What did he *have*? The farm would go to one of his older brothers. His sisters would be married out. One of his brothers had married a girl with a prosperous father—the dowry was his farm. But the next brother would expect to get Father's farm, in due time. What would any of the younger boys have? He had known this without knowing he knew it.

Was that why he had taken it into his head to walk over the Mitherkame to this place? It must have been.

The hand on his shoulder relaxed. "It's not a light thing, serving a mage," he said, as Runnel turned to face him. The man was tall and swarthy—a man of the south, like some of the travelers that had passed through Farzibeck.

"So you're no man's prentice?" asked Demwor.

"We're all farmers in Farzibeck," said Runnel.

"No smith? No harness maker?"

"We make our own harnesses. We work in stone and wood. We drink the water Yeggut gives us and we eat what Yeggut makes to grow from the earth. I've heard of prentices because some of the travelers have them, but I couldn't figure how they were different from slaves."

"The difference," said Demwor, "is that the master pays for the slave, but to take a prentice, the father pays the master to take him. That's how useless prentices are, and why Master Brickel will never, never, *never* take a prentice."

"That's good news to me," said Runnel, "because I'd never want to be taken for a prentice."

"Just so you understand," said Demwor. "We'd hire you as a servant only. Base labor, you understand. There'll be manure, there'll be slops, there'll be backbreaking work with stone, there'll be burdens."

That described the life of everybody in Farzibeck, including the stones, which they had to haul out of their fields every spring, after the winter heaved them up to snag the plow. "I'm not afraid of work, sir."

"Then I have only one more question," said Demwor. "How do you feel about stone?"

Feel? About stone? What was he supposed to *feel* about it? "I'm in favor of it for walls," said Runnel, "and against it for soil."

Demwor chuckled. "You have a proud face," he said, "but a humble wit."

"The face is not my fault," said Runnel. "Nor is my wit, since I was born with both, and both are humble enough, sir."

"What I ask about stone is simple. Have you worked in stone? Have you built with stone? Have you shaped it?"

"Is it required? Because I can learn if you want. But no, I've never worked stone. We just find it and make barriers sometimes, to slacken the floods of spring in a heavy snow year. And the foundations of our hovels are of stone pressed into the earth. But I've never actually helped to build such, since no hovel has been built since I've been big enough."

"It is not required," said Demwor, "and we don't want you to learn it."

"Then I won't," said Runnel.

"Because if you think you can try to learn magic from Master Brickel, I can tell you that you *will* be detected, and it will go hard for you."

"Magic?" said Runnel. "How can I learn magic? I'm no mage."

"Just remember that," said Demwor, "and you won't get this house into trouble."

"The house? Your master *is* a stonemage."

"No, lad," said Demwor. "My master is *the* stonemage. The only one permitted to enter Mitherhome. The only one allowed within this whole valley. And *he* is sworn never to learn new magicks, beyond what he knew when he came here. Stonemage he is, but not a rockbrother, and especially not a stonefather. He's a cobblefriend, which is all the power needed for the work he does here. That is why the watermages of Mitherhome pay him so handsomely, and provide him this house—because he hasn't the power to do us harm."

And suddenly it became clear to Runnel. Demwor didn't work for Brickel, he worked for the Mithermages. Yes, he saw to the affairs of Brickel's household and hired the servants and paid for the food, but he was also Brickel's overseer, making sure Brickel did not break the terms of his oath. Without even meeting him, Runnel felt a little sorry for Brickel.

But not *too* sorry. Because here the man lived with wealth—servants, a garden courtyard ten times larger than the hovel where Runnel's huge family slept, all the food he needed.

"Sir," said Runnel, "my aim in life is to earn enough to eat and a place to sleep and maybe a little of this money everyone wants so much. So Lark is safe, and you are safe, and your master is safe, and your city is safe from my ambition, because I'm little and ignorant and hungry and tired. But if you take care of the hungry and tired, you'll find me big enough to do whatever work you need, and I'll only get bigger, because all my older brothers are as tall as soldiers, and so is my father, and my mother isn't tiny by any measure."

Demwor burst into laughter. "I've never heard such a sales pitch—and from such a serious face, too. I take you at your word, boy. What's your name again?"

"Runnel, sir."

"Start thinking of what you want to change it to," said Demwor.

"I won't, sir."

"We can't have the stonemage's servant with a water name, lest the people think he's mocking them."

"He's not my father, he hired me is all," said Runnel. "So no one with half a wit will think he's responsible for my name."

"But he hasn't hired you, and he won't, with a name like that."

"Then I thank you for the water, sir," said Runnel. "But I didn't come here to be any man's slave, nor to give up my name neither."

"Who said anything about a slave?"

"It's the owner of a slave who gets to change his name, sir," said Runnel. "I know *that* because the three old servants in Farzibeck were given new names when they were taken captive in war."

Demwor shook his head. "So that pride in your face isn't all illusion, is it? Too proud to change your name in exchange for a job."

"Not proud, sir," said Runnel. "But Runnel of Farzibeck won't die here to have a waterless coward rise in his place."

"Waterless coward?" said Demwor. "Farzibeck—it's in the mountains, is it?"

"West of here, along the Utteroad," said Runnel. "Just beyond the pass over the Mitherkame."

"So you're named Runnel out of piety. You serve Yeggut?"

"I come here to find I may be the only one who does," said Runnel.

Demwor put a hand on his shoulder once more, and Runnel flinched, but the hand was kindly this time. "You'll do, I think," said Demwor. "A boy from a mountain village, with a watername that means devotion, not ambition. Yes, that's better. You were right to stand your ground, and not give up the name."

Demwor patted his shoulder and walked back toward the house.

Lark wasn't having that. "Is he hired then, sir?"

"Yes," said Demwor.

"What's his wage?" she demanded.

"Same as yours," said Demwor.

"That's not right!" she shouted. "I've worked here two years already!"

"But *he* carried the waterjar full." And Demwor was gone into the house.

Lark was furious. "*Drown* him and all his kittens," she muttered fiercely.

"He hired me," said Runnel.

"At far more wage than you're worth," she said.

"If you like, I'll give you part of it, since you brought me here."

For a moment her eyes lighted up. And then she backed away. "I won't have no man thinking I owe him."

Runnel shook his head. "Your precious treasure is safe from me," he said. "I owe *you*, for bringing me here."

"I thought you'd almost ruined everything, when you refused to change your name."

"It turned out all right," said Runnel.

"How did you know it would?" she asked.

"I didn't."

"So you *meant* all that?" She seemed astonished.

"It's my *name*," said Runnel.

"You are the most ignorant person I've ever known. What's a name?"

"You guard *your* purity," said Runnel, "and I guard mine."

Here eyes and nostrils flared and she swung as if to slap him, but then she didn't actually hit him. Nor, however, did he flinch. "Don't you ever dare to compare your *name* with my *purity,* as you call it. Someday I mean to earn my dowry and *marry,* not be some kitchen slut making coin on the side or winning favor from the master or the steward. Purity *is* the only treasure that a poor girl has, which is why I took this job, because people leave me alone, which means I have hope. While your name—it's not famous, it's not important, it's *worthless.* So don't you dare compare them again, ever!"

She stalked away from him, into the house, leaving him to finish his water, which he did.

What's worthless to you might not be worthless to me, he said silently. But he couldn't help feeling disappointed. Somehow he had managed to lose her friendship after all. It would be just like home.

He leaned against the cistern and closed his eyes. He had a job. He would be paid money. He had no idea what money was worth but he was being paid the same as Lark, and *she* believed it was enough that she could save up a dowry.

She was young, and might be counting on ten years or more to build up what she wanted. But he was even younger, and could work longer before marrying. As a farmer, he had only just started doing men's work, and not yet the full range of that. But here, he would learn everything and grow into whatever jobs were too hard for him.

Lots of hard work. Years of it. Why was he so excited?

It was because he would be with a stonemage. What did he care if he was only a cobblefriend and not one of the higher orders? He might even see magic done.

Meanwhile, there were practical benefits. Like this cistern. He could feel how it worked inside—the water in the tank above seeped right through a porous stone that trapped anything that shouldn't be in it. It was slow for the water to seep its way through the rock, but all impurities were removed—ironic that the purest, cleanest water in Hetterferry should be in the stonemage's house.

The porous stone was a surprise, though. He had never known rock like this, not in any of the outcroppings he had climbed. He wished it were outside the cistern where he could get his hands on it. If only *he* were a stonemage so he could understand how the filtering worked.

Dangerous thought. He must not wish to be a stonemage. He had taken an oath not to become one. If Demwor hadn't made such a fuss about how he shouldn't be one, he wouldn't be wishing he could be one right now.

It didn't matter. Mages were magical people, not ordinary farmboys. Mages could go out into the world in the shape of their beloved—beast mages as the beast they favored, elemental mages in bodies of stone or wind or water, lightning or sand or metal. They could not be confined, not the ones with real power. Runnel imagined himself as a stonemage like Brickel, his new master. He could walk the earth in a stone body, and then what weapon could harm him?

I hope I can see my master in his stoneshape. Or must he keep such things secret, because Demwor was here to watch?

"Runnel," said an impatient voice. "What are you doing?"

He opened his eyes and saw Lark standing there again.

"Finishing my water," he said.

"Without the beaker in your hand? What do you do, suck it up through your ears?"

Don't be angry with me, he wanted to say. But he hesitated, and she talked again.

"Do you think you're going to live out here in the garden? Come with me. I'm supposed to show you your room."

Runnel dutifully followed her into the house. She walked briskly, so he scarcely had time to notice the different rooms or try to guess what they were used for. His family's hovel was one room, with a chimney at one end. He had no idea why so many rooms would be needed; they did not look convenient for sleeping, there was so much furniture in odd shapes. Tall boxes with doors all up and down them. Tables with cloth covering them, and so bumpy that you couldn't possibly get any work done on them. Until he realized that they were really huge, wide chairs, and the cloth was there to cover the wood so it wouldn't hurt to sit a long time. Cloth, just to dress chairs and make them soft! No one in Farzibeck would even have understood it.

They went up a flight of narrow wooden stairs. "Why didn't we use the wide stairs in the front?" asked Runnel.

She didn't answer.

He sighed. So much for the hope that she might forgive him for what was, after all, an unintentional offense.

"Always use these stairs," she finally said. "The front stairs are for the master, Demwor, and guests. Servants use the back stairs."

So decency and good order had prevailed over temper. She didn't want him getting in trouble because she never told him about the stairs rule. That was almost...compassionate.

Up two, three flights, to the very top of the house. And then up another even narrower stairway to a room where the walls and roof were the rafters.

He had never climbed so high inside a building. Farzibeck had only one barn as tall as this, and he wasn't allowed inside it. He had gone once anyway, with a group of his brothers, but they wouldn't let him climb a ladder and he hadn't wanted to anyway. It's not that he was afraid of heights—he could climb as high as he wanted, outdoors. But going up the stairs he felt as though he were climbing right up into the air, leaving the solid earth too far behind him.

Three floors between him and the earth, each one shakier than the one before. He felt as thought the house were swaying. He hated the feeling. "We have to sleep up *here*?"

"Too proud?" she asked pointedly.

"Too scared," he said. "What holds us up?"

She looked at him as if he were crazy. "The walls of the house, the floors." She touched one of the heavy rafters. "Huge beams of heavy wood."

"It trembles."

"It does *not*," she said, as if he had just accused her of something.

He tried to think of some rational basis for his discomfort. "It can fall. It can burn. I want to sleep outside on the stone flags of the courtyard."

"Do you want to shame our master by making people believe he doesn't have enough rooms for his servants to sleep in?"

"Who would know?" asked Runnel.

She apparently had no answer, so she glared at him. "Take it up with Demwor. I took you where he said you should go."

She started for the stairs.

Runnel hated that she was so angry with him. "Please, Lark," he said. "If I *do* ask him to let me sleep in the courtyard —"

She answered him scornfully before he could even finish his question. "What do *you* think happens to a servant who makes trouble on his first day?"

Since he had never had a paying job, working for strangers, the fear of being dismissed from his position had never occurred to him. The most he had feared was a blow or two—he knew, from life with Father, that he could easily cope with that. But he could not take the chance of giving up this place.

He didn't even know whether this was a good place to work or not—there were probably reasons why this house did not have enough servants and needed to hire a stray freshly arrived from the mountains. It was his own problem that sleeping three floors above the ground bothered him. Other people did it. He would have to get over being such a mountain boy and learn to live in a town.

As all this dawned on him, Lark's expression showed such contempt for him that it was like a slap. "Whose face is proud *now*?" he asked her.

She whirled her head away from him and went on down the stairs. He could hear the soft sliding of the soles of her bare feet on the wood. It was a sound he didn't like. It made him shiver. Feet were meant to walk on grass or soil or hard-packed dirt or stone, not on trees sliced up and laid out sideways. It was unnatural.

He surveyed the straw-filled tick that was apparently meant to be his bed. Even in the scant light coming into the attic through cracks in the eaves, he could see that there were fleas jumping on it. He had nothing against fleas, he just couldn't imagine how they had stayed alive with no one else sleeping up in this hot space.

Then it all came clear. Someone *had* been living up here until just recently. These were his leftover fleas. If he had happened along just a bit earlier or later, the job would have been taken.

He wondered why his predecessor had been dismissed. He asked to sleep on the ground? Or he tried to learn magery? Or he spoke slightingly of Lark's purity? Any of these offenses seemed near fatal, as far as Runnel could tell.

Since it was still broad daylight outside, and he hadn't eaten anything, and neither had anyone else, judging by the smells coming from a kitchen somewhere on the property, he figured he wasn't meant to try to sleep right now, though he was tired enough. If he was to get along well here, he'd need to show himself a hard worker—that was about the only thing that could ever postpone Father's wrath, so it was worth trying here.

The trouble was, he had no idea what tasks he ought to do. Nor did he want to bother anybody with asking. But unless he asked, he'd…

No point in thinking any longer. He headed for the stairs and set his foot on the second-from-top step and felt it tremble under him and all at once he was as dizzy as if he'd just spun in circles for a dozen turns, the way they all used to do as little kids, until somebody threw up.

He sat on the top step. There was no railing. Going up had been easy enough—he only had to keep his eyes on Lark ahead of him, a sight that was engaging enough that he hadn't really been aware of the drop-off on either side. Now, though, he had neither companion nor handrail nor distraction, and he was only able to make his way down the stairs by sitting on a tread, extending his legs to a lower one, then sliding his buttocks down to the next step.

The rest of the stairs were much easier, since there was a wall on one side or the other, and a railing as well. But the house never stopped trembling and Runnel never felt secure until he was on the ground floor.

Which was foolish, he knew, since there was a cellar beneath this floor, so it wasn't truly the *ground* under his feet even now. But being level with the ground seemed to be enough. Maybe it was just that the floor beams rested on stone foundations, instead of wooden walls.

How would he find out what work he ought to do? Without asking Lark or bothering Demwor? It was easy to guess that he shouldn't go in search of Lord Brickel.

He ended up following his nose to the kitchen, a stone building behind the main house—far enough that if the kitchen burnt down it wouldn't take the house with it, but close enough that hot food would still be hot when served, even after being carried through the coldest weather.

The cook turned out to be cooks: A tall, lean black man and a fleshy woman with slanting eyes. As he approached the kitchen, Runnel could hear him calling her Sourwell—a water name—and her calling him Nikwiz, which wasn't a word he knew, any more than Demwor's name had meant anything to him. Their tones were quiet, and when Runnel entered the fire-dried room—so hot that he thought having an oven was redundant—they ignored him and kept speaking to each other.

"Ready for that."

"Steady with the salt."

"Taste it, you'll see."

"Old."

"But edible."

"Perfect."

If Runnel hadn't been watching, it wouldn't even have sounded like a conversation, but he could see that "ready for that" led to her handing him what looked like a large spoon, but with holes in the bottom so that when he shook it over the steaming pot, white granules came out. "Steady with the salt" was said after he made his second pass with the shaker. "Taste it, you'll see," led to Sourwell dipping a finger into Nikwiz's pot as she passed on an errand of her own; she nodded and he made yet another pass with the shaker.

"Old," she said when she picked up a couple of turnips and eyed them skeptically. He didn't even look—he was busy now mincing an onion—so he must have bought the turnips, because his "but edible" sounded authoritative. By then she was on to the oven, where she slid out a long tray with two round loaves on it—"perfect" was pronounced as judgment on the bread.

Neither of them had yet shown a sign of knowing Runnel was there, but as Nikwiz scattered the onions into a hot pan, making the grease in it sizzle, he said, "If you've come to beg for scraps, no. If you've come to steal, I promise you dysentery."

"I've just been hired, and I came to ask if you've any work for me," said Runnel. "My name is Runnel."

"Can you cook?" asked Sourwell.

"Anyone can cook," said Nikwiz. "You just climb into the oven."

It took a moment for Runnel to realize that this was a joke—Sourwell didn't even break a smile, and yet Runnel could see that both she and Nikwiz were both shaking with mirth at the remark.

"My mother never let me near the cooking. Or knives. My sisters —"

"Fascinating," said Sourwell in a tone that meant the opposite.

"Put the owl on the roof," said Nikwiz, "to scare the birds and mice away."

And they were back to cooking.

I'm supposed to catch an owl? Or is there a tame one?

"Outside," said Sourwell. "Blew off in the last storm."

He went out and walked almost all the way around the kitchen building before he found a carved stone owl leaning against a wall. It was cunningly shaped, and it had been daubed with paint to make it more convincing to birds and mice, though Runnel wondered whether those beasts were really that stupid.

The owl was also very heavy. He realized at once that they expected him to be too small to manage it.

But the end walls of the kitchen were stone all the way up, gables and all, the thatch of the roof resting between them like hay in a manger. The owl must rest on the peak of the stone gable—and now that he looked, he could see that another owl rested on the peak of the other end of the kitchen.

Tucking the owl against his body, Runnel had a tough go of it, climbing up the stone wall one-handed, but with bare feet he managed it well enough, and within two minutes after picking up the owl, he was back down, with the owl perched menacingly atop the crest of the kitchen.

He went back inside. "What next?" he asked.

"We didn't ask you to *find* the owl," said Sourwell. "We need it put atop the roof."

"Did it," said Runnel. "What else?"

As if it were part of her regular routine, Sourwell swept out of the kitchen and in a moment came back in and resumed her cooking. In a perfectly mild voice she said, "Singe my sockets, but the boy must fly."

"Bet he left the ladder outside to rot," said Nikwiz.

"Ladder?" asked Runnel.

Their smooth dance of food preparation finally came to a halt, as both of them looked for a long moment at Runnel, then at each other. "Break eggs much?" asked Nikwiz.

"Prone to spilling things?" asked Sourwell.

"No more than most," said Runnel. "I'm not careless, but I'm not perfect."

"We wanted perfect," said Nikwiz, visibly disappointed.

"Best use me for jobs that can be done by the less-than-perfect," said Runnel.

"Here," said Sourwell, slapping a knife down on a cutting stone and pointing to a pile of peppers. "Don't cut yourself."

For the next hour, Runnel chopped and minced peppers and onions on smooth-cut slabs of granite. He quickly learned not to rub his eyes. He cried a lot and sneezed now and then. His eyes burned. He was useful. He was earning his keep.

Then they kicked him out of the kitchen with orders to wash his hands with soap three times before washing his face—again with soap—to clear the last of the onion and pepper residues from his face. "Scrub," said Sourwell. "Hard," said Nikwiz. "Never a soapmage where you need one," added Sourwell.

"I never heard of soapmages," said Runnel.

"Me neither," said Nikwiz. "Go wash."

He found a washbasin outside the kitchen, made of stone, of course. He rocked the small cistern and filled the basin with water, then lathered his hands with one of the cakes of hard soap. He was scrubbing his face, including especially his closed eyes, when he heard voices.

"Doesn't look like much," said an old man.

"Isn't much," said Demwor. "But he made himself useful in the kitchen this afternoon without being ordered."

"All arse and elbows," said the old man. "And what is he *wearing*?"

"The latest in mountain village fashions," said Demwor.

It had to be Lord Brickel himself that Demwor was talking to, and Runnel wanted to see him, but he couldn't see anything until he rinsed his face, and thoroughly. By the time he was able to towel himself on his shirt and turn around, he could just see them disappearing into the house.

He didn't see him at supper, either. Lord Brickel ate with company in his dining room; Runnel ate at the big table in the kitchen with the other servants, of whom there were only the ones he'd already seen: Demwor, Nikwiz, Sourwell, and Ebb, the stupid man from the doorway.

Demwor, Nikwiz, and Sourwell kept up a constant conversation about the business of the house and gossip in the neighborhood. Ebb said nothing, which is what Runnel said as well.

Lark was waiting table tonight so she was in and out of the kitchen, and she certainly didn't speak to Runnel.

"Going to buy the new one something respectable to wear?" asked Sourwell.

"Wasn't thinking of it," said Demwor. "He's not naked. He's not going out on errands for the house."

"He'll have to wear something when she washes his clothes," pointed out Sourwell.

The mentioned "she" had to be Lark. Runnel was sure Lark would be thrilled to know she'd be doing that chore.

"I can wash my own," said Runnel. "If you show me where."

"It talks," said Nikwiz.

"With its mouth full," said Sourwell.

They didn't smile and nobody laughed, but Runnel knew he was being teased, and with good humor. It felt good.

"Take him to market with you tomorrow," said Demwor, "and buy him something that fits. I'll take it out of his earnings. But if he runs off and takes the new clothes before they're earned out, I'll dock *your* wages."

"Just try it," said Nikwiz.

"When we prepare every bite of food you eat," said Sourwell.

"What kind of household is this," said Demwor. "Two cooks, one smart-mouthed girl, a mountain bumpkin, and a cheerful dolt."

"You're forgetting Ebb," said Nikwiz.

It took a moment for Runnel to get the gibe; he laughed aloud.

Demwor glared at him. "Don't get the idea that I'll let *you* speak disrespectfully to me, boy, just because I let the cooks do it."

"No sir," said Runnel.

"And you'll wash those clothes and bathe yourself tonight. With soap! I won't have you bringing fleas into the house."

Which explained why Lark's clothing was so clean. Demwor insisted on it.

"Where do I wash them?" asked Runnel. "Since there's no stream close by."

"The washbasin is at the west corner of the garden," said Nikwiz.

"Carry your own water there," said Sourwell.

"There's a stove out there for heating the water," said Demwor, "but if you break a jar from overheating it or setting it cold on a hot stove, I'll dock you."

Runnel had no idea what "docking" him might mean, but he was sure it was something he wanted to avoid having done either to him or his wages. But that was all right. He had never heard of heating water for washing clothes. And only Father washed in hot water back home, and only in winter.

After supper he found the laundry tub, estimated how much water he'd need to wash and rinse the clothes and himself, and then carried a large jar of water from the main cistern. He stripped off his clothes and put them in the water, then soaped them on the washboard.

"You nasty boy!" said Lark behind him. Her voice was full of revulsion.

"I haven't washed myself yet," he answered.

"I don't care that you're dirty, stupid. You're *naked*."

"Excuse me, I didn't think of washing my clothes with me still in them," said Runnel.

"Do you always do your laundry naked back in Farzibeck?" she said snidely.

"Yes," he said. "It's that or sit naked in the house like a baby while somebody else washes them. Only in Farzibeck, the girls have sense enough to stay away while the boys are laundering, and we boys'd be killed if we walked up on the girls like you just walked up on me." This was not strictly true. When boys got their man growth, they would keep a loincloth on. But Runnel had not started wearing one yet.

"I have laundry to do," said Lark. "For the master."

"Then you can either wait till later, or you can do it with your eyes closed, because I'm not leaving here till my clothes and my body are clean."

"Dry! It'll take forever for your clothes to dry!"

"Dry?" asked Runnel. "Where will they dry, except on *me*?"

"I'm not going to go to bed late because you picked *this* moment to discover cleanliness."

"Demwor told me to wash clothes and boy," said Runnel. "And the reason I was so dirty was because I had just taken a journey along roads and through woods, and slept in leaves on the forest floor. Next time I'll remember to have someone carry me in a litter or pull me in a carriage."

She set down a full basket of white linens.

"The master must wear a lot of white," said Runnel.

"This is his underwear, mountain boy," she said contemptuously. "Obviously you've never heard of it."

It was a strange world, indeed, for a man to have underwear like a baby—and a whole basketful at that.

Lark poured the rest of the water from his jar into the tub and dropped a cake of soap in with it. Then she took the washboard from Runnel's side of the tub and began scrubbing the linens.

"I guess my clothes are clean enough now," said Runnel, getting up.

"Don't stand up!" she said. "Don't you have *any* modesty?"

"You just poured out the rinse water," said Runnel. "I have to get more."

"You should have brought more water in the first place," she said.

"I brought enough water for my body and my clothes to be washed and rinsed," he said. "You brought none." He picked up the empty jar and headed back across the garden to the courtyard where the cistern waited.

The jar was almost half-full when Demwor came up to him. "In this house we wear clothing," he said sharply.

Runnel bit back all his two possible answers: "I'm not *in* the house" would get him slapped or kicked out for insolence. "You told me to wash my clothes when you knew I didn't have any others" was likely to get the same result. So instead he said, "I had to replenish the water so Lark could do the laundry."

"So you were naked with Lark?" Demwor's expression turned furious.

He could not leave that one unanswered. "I was naked alone with a laundry tub! *She* decided she had to do her laundry right then and use up all the water I brought. I had to get more so I could rinse my clothes because not even for *you* am I putting them back on with soap still in them!"

Demwor at first got angrier, but then calmed himself. "You could have left your underwear on until your outerwear was clean."

Runnel just sighed.

"Don't have underwear?" Now Demwor was amused.

"I'm not a baby," said Runnel.

That was apparently the funniest thing of all. But after one bark of laughter, he was back to chiding. "We don't do our laundry in the filtered water." He showed Runnel the tap that drew water directly from the cistern without passing through the porous stone first. It flowed much more readily, and the jar was quickly full.

"He's naked!" said Ebb cheerfully when Demwor passed him on the way back to the house.

So Runnel had learned something else—people went insane when you took your clothes off. In the village, clothing was for *warmth*. Only girls worried about modesty, and only when they got near that age. During summer, men often worked naked in the fields. It was part of life; during hot weather, a man would strip himself as surely as he'd shear the sheep. What did they do here in the city? *Sweat* in their clothing so it would stink? No wonder they had to wash all the time.

He carried the full waterjar back to the laundry. Lark was still scrubbing linens. He tipped all the water out of the tub onto the stone flags of the washing pit. Lark leapt to her feet with a cry, then began picking up linens. "Now I have to wash them again, you fool! You oaf!"

"You felt free to take my water and the washboard from *me*," said Runnel. "That's how I thought things were done."

"I'm doing the master's laundry!"

"And I'm doing the laundry that Demwor told *me* to do," he said. "You're the one who decided to be mean. If you want to get along with me, then treat me fairly. I'll do the same in return. But right now, I'm rinsing my clothes. And washing and rinsing myself. Then you can do what you like."

Only then did he see that she had already slopped his clothes out of the tub and tossed them, not onto the clean flagstones, but out into the dirt. She saw where he was looking and she blushed. That was all he needed—he knew she was sorry for having caused him extra work.

"Thank you for helping me get this position," he said. "Even if you punish me the rest of my life for saying one wrong thing without meaning any harm, and for washing clothes the way we do it in the mountains, I'll still thank you for helping me get a place here. I'm in your debt, and I won't do anything like pouring out your washwater again. I'm sorry for that. It wasn't right."

As he spoke, he went for his clothes and brought them back to the tub. By now she was pouring water in, her lips set and her eyes downcast. He put his clothes back in the tub and knelt to wash them again. But she held onto the washboard and began scrubbing his clothing herself.

"I'll do it," he said.

But she ignored him and scrubbed.

"I don't want you serving me," he said.

"Go stand behind something till I have your clothes clean," she said irritably. "Pretend to be decent."

He obeyed and leaned against the stone wall of the garden, with a tree between him and her. He thought of climbing the wall to see what was on the other side, but decided that nude wall-climbing wasn't in the spirit of decency that she had in mind. He could hear her wringing out his wet clothes and spattering water on the pavement.

After a while she brought his trousers and tunic and, still averting her eyes, offered them to him. He took the shirt and pulled it on over his head. "I'm covered now," he said.

"Just take your pants," she said.

He took them, but didn't fasten them with the cord; they'd stay up well enough, being damp, and it wouldn't do to tie the cord wet or he'd never get it off. He went back to the washtub as soon as he was dressed.

"Go away," she said.

"Lark," he said. "I don't ask you to be my friend. Just let me help you do your work faster, since I delayed you."

"I do this job myself."

"I can wring out the linens," said Runnel. "I can pour water, even if you don't let me scrub."

In reply, she handed him a pair of underdrawers to wring. He did, and draped it where she pointed, on one of several strings between two tree limbs.

After most of the linens were hanging, she finally spoke to him. "It was a waste of time, you know, putting that stupid owl back up on the kitchen roof."

"Doesn't it work?"

"The mice live inside the kitchen walls and never *see* the owl," she said. "And no birds come here."

"Doesn't that mean that it *does* work?"

"It means no birds come over these walls, whether there's an owl or not."

"Why not?"

"Because they'd expect me to feed them and care for them and I can't," she said. "So I ask them not to come." She looked up at him defiantly.

He nodded gravely. "You're a birdfriend, then."

"I'm no mage of any kind," she said. "I just get along with birds."

"Birdfriend," he said, "but I won't tell."

"It's one of the reasons it's so hard for them to find servants here. Nobody likes to admit they've got no magery, not even a scrap. First thing people do is show off, or brag if they've got nought to show. Even though birdmagery has nothing to do with stone, and birdmages aren't forbidden to enter Mitherhome any way. Makes no sense and does no harm, but Demwor won't have a mage of any kind in the household."

"For fear they'll learn stonemagic?"

"It's because of the great war," she said. "When the soldiers of Veryllydd came to try to force Mitherhome to become part of the empire of Yllydd again, and the watermages here said no, for when Yllydd was a great empire, it was Mydderllydd that ruled it, and Veryllydd was subject to *them* then."

Runnel could tell that it was a story she had committed to memory, especially because she pronounced the "ll" of Yllydd in the old way, that hissing sound from the sides of the tongue when it was forming an "L." It was the language of stories. Though he hoped it wouldn't be too long. He was very tired. Also, having drunk much at supper, he needed to pee.

"The armies of Veryllydd had their mages of light and mages of metal, for in those days Mitherhome had only swords of obsidian to raise in battle. Thus in the day, the blood of the holy forest was soaked with the blood of heroes. And at night, the lightmages made the night of their tunnels into day, so they sapped under the mighty western walls of Mitherhome."

Runnel felt a chill as he realized that this was the explanation for the broken walls he had seen, approaching the city from the west. The blood of heroes: That was why the western forest was sacred, and no one built there.

"The elders of the city knew the western approach was their great weakness, so they built the second wall at the foot of the Mitherjut. This, too, the Verylludden sapped, and the doom of the Mitherfolk was plain for all to see.

"Now came the stonemages of Mitherhome, who had once ruled all of Mydderllyd before the waterfolk conquered them long before. 'We do not wish to be ruled by Veryllydd,' they said. 'We can stop them: Rockbrother and cobblefriend, we shall do it.'"

"Then the stonemages went to the peak of Mitherjut, where once their ancient temple stood. They bared again the rocks of the holy place, and lay naked upon the stone, and the rock-brothers sank into it as the cobblefriends sang. First their temple arose, new and whole, made not of blocks like the temples of all other folk, but of living stone thrust up until rockbrother and cobblefriend were entirely surrounded by their temple, with neither door nor window in the dome. Now they were surrounded by stone, almost as if they were stonefathers who can move within the living rock.

"The Verylludden sappers set fire to the beams in their tunnels, and the inner wall of the city trembled and began to fall. But as it fell, lo! A great cleft opened in the earth, from the Mitherlough to the river below, cleaving the Veryllydd army in twain. Many fell into the great crevice, including all the lightmages, as the waters of the lake swept into the breach, forming a new channel, the Stonemages' Ditch, flowing down to the river, making Mitherhome into an island with water on all sides. Now no need of walls! The portion of the Verylludden on this side of the crevice were pushed back and cast into the cleft; the army on the other side screamed and wept and pleaded as the ground beneath them shook so no man could stand.

"A great bridge grew from the hither side of the Stonemages' Ditch to the yon, and the army of Mydderllydd crossed over to wreak havoc on those who would have destroyed them. Now, with the hearts of the stonemages in them, the stone swords of the Mydderfolk cut the bronze swords of the mighty Veryllydd like new cheese, and their blood flowed like water, until ten times as many Verylludden died there as they had killed before. So many were dead within the broken outer walls of the city that you could walk from wall to Ditch without stepping on the ground." She stopped and bowed her head, for all the world like a traveling talespinner. For such a tale as that, a traveler could earn a meal and a bed for the night; she had told it well.

"I walked that ground just yesterday, and slept there, and woke this morning in that wood," said Runnel in reverent tones.

She looked at him wide-eyed. "Were the bodies there?"

"Covered with leaves and soil, maybe," he said. "I didn't see any. But Lark, if the stonemages saved the city, why have they been banned? Why are they not welcomed as brothers?"

"That's the sad part of the story," said Lark. "I never like to hear it, but I learned it, if you must have the telling."

"Please," he said.

"The rulers of the city went to the great cleft, and saw the torrent of water that formed a little lake, and then tumbled down the canyon to the river below, and they said, 'This new outflow will drain our lake, and leave Yeggut diminished so he will no longer bless us.'

"Now it happened that the stonemages had foreseen this, and raised stone on the other side to reduce the outflow there, so the lake level was unchanged. The water mages knew this, for the water told them so, but they feared the power of the stonemages to steal their water. 'Today they were our friends,' said the watermages. 'But tomorrow, what if they remember that Mitherhome was once Mydderstane, built by stonemages and conquered by latecome watermen? They will say, "It is ours by right," and they will destroy us as they destroyed the Veryludden.'

"So in fear of the power of the stonemages, the rulers caused great heaps of wood to be piled all round the solid living temple that contained the great mages who had saved them, and they lit the fire, which heated the temple until the stone glowed red. Nothing could live inside it. For two days the fire burnt, and then it died, yet for five more days no man could touch the stone.

"When the rock at last was cool, the rulers of the city caused the dome to be broken open, and inside were found ashes in the shape of each of the stonemages; even their bones were ash. The watermages called water up through the rock and it flowed from the center of the temple, so it became a spring, holy to Yeggut, and not an outcropping of stone.

"Then the temple was broken entirely apart and the pieces carried down and cast into the cleft. The bridge of living stone was broken apart, for it was said that the stonemages had done this to turn the new channel into a tunnel, with living stone all around it. It was decreed that forever no bridge would span that cleft." She broke off the narrative. "That's why Hetterferry came to exist."

"It's a sad story," said Runnel. "And it doesn't make the watermages of the city sound very noble, to murder the very folk who saved them."

"That's not how the tale is told in Mitherhome, I'm sure," said Lark. "But it's how I learned it, back in the —"

"It's a pack of lies," said Demwor.

Runnel whirled to look at him. He was very angry.

"She only told it as she learned it, sir," said Runnel.

"She doesn't need you to defend her," said Demwor. "I see now why she came to work at a stonemage's house."

"No, sir," she said. "I came because the work was good and safe. I learned this story as a child, it's a children's tale."

"Then listen to me well, *children.* Tell this tale no more, not to anyone. It's a slander of the stonemages against our city. They were traitors, that's the truth, in league with our enemies."

"Then why would they make the cleft that keeps the city safe?" asked Runnel.

"They didn't!" shouted Demwor. Then, more softly: "It has always been there. Their plot was to deepen it until it drained the lake and our enemies could get through on dry land. They were barely stopped in time."

"Thank you for telling us the truth, sir," said Runnel. Well he knew that the only way to stave off a beating was to agree quickly with the man who was raging. "We'll never tell it the other way again. Forgive us for being ignorant children from far away, where truth disappears inside extravagant tales." It was something his mother had once said, that bit about truth disappearing inside tales—only she had said it about gossip that had a village girl pregnant by a god, instead of by a traveler who gave her a golden fruit that was full of sweet water.

Demwor peered into Runnel's face, and then Lark's, looking for something—defiance, perhaps. But both of them looked as abject as any ruler could ask, and finally he said, "Your chatter has made you late to bed. I'll have you up as early as ever tomorrow, you understand? And still you must finish washing and wringing and hanging the master's linens."

"Almost done," said Lark. "I kept working while I talked."

"I saw you from the second story of the house, and you were working slowly. That's why I came out here."

Runnel said nothing more, only bowed. He half expected Demwor to cuff him once or twice, just because he had been angry—that's what Father did. Runnel even placed himself between Demwor and Lark, so that if he was one who struck out in his wrath, the blows would fall only on Runnel.

But there were no blows. Demwor walked away, and Runnel and Lark hurriedly finished the rinsing and wringing and hanging. Then Runnel carried what was left of the water back to the cistern, where he poured it back into the top, where it could join the water yet to be filtered. Nothing wasted...only the soapy water had been poured out onto the stones; the rinse water was cast into the vegetable garden. "We grow the cleanest radishes and yams," said Lark, but her smile was wan.

"We'll speak no more of your tale," said Runnel. "Your malicious, false, and unbelievable slander. Except to say that I looked down into the crevice, and some malicious, false, and deceptive slanderer has cast stones into the canyon and created the ruins of a nonexistent bridge, just so people will *think* your version of the tale is true."

She smiled at him. "You're a complete fool, Runnel. I forgive you for mocking me even after we took an oath."

"I meant no mockery…"

But she was already gone.

Runnel went to the pissery, where urine was saved, and contributed his few ounces to some future slab of soap. Then he went to the cistern and drank again, so he wouldn't waken with thirst in the night. But not too much, so he wouldn't waken with a full bladder.

Mostly, though, he was putting off the climb up those stairs, to try to sleep at the top of a swaying, shaking building. I know how those Verylludden felt, with the ground shaking under them and their bronze swords turning to cheese.

Inside the house, though, all was still. Wherever Lark slept, she must be there; Ebb, he knew, slept by the door in the outer wall. Demwor might be awake but he wasn't on watch on the lower floor.

I can say that I didn't want to wake anybody by climbing the stair as they were trying to sleep.

It was a feeble plan, and he knew it—but having formed the idea, he acted on it at once. He found the steps leading down into the cellar.

It was dark, like a cloudy, moonless night. Even after waiting, his eyes still could not find light enough to make out anything at all.

His toes, though, found the stone flags of the floor easily enough. But there was something wrong—the stones were trembling almost as much as the wood of the upper stories had been. They also gave under his feet, shifting with his weight. Finally he realized: They had been laid across wood.

The watermages are so frightened even of this one stone-mage that not only do they have Demwor to keep watch over the house, but also they have cut off the stone of the house from the living rock of the earth.

They're afraid that even from here, Lord Brickel may be able to do some terrible thing to the stone underlying their city—or, more to the point, the channels through which their precious water flowed.

Well, it *is* precious water, thought Runnel. Six hours without water and I begin to thirst. But when have I ever needed stone to slake my desire? If you have to choose between Tewstan and Yeggut, it was Yeggut who sustained life minute by minute and hour by hour.

Though if Tewstan hated you, where would you be safe from his wrath?

Not here in this cellar. You could put wood between the flagstones and the living stone below, but they could not have done that with the walls of the cellar, because they were holding up the upper floors. Walls had to touch the living stone or the house could not stand.

Sure enough, the foundation of the great hearth of the common room above was stone that connect fully to the living rock; it was here that Runnel made his bed, his hand touching the stone of the foundation. Here alone the house did not tremble. Here alone he could sleep with the same ease he felt on the packed-earth floor of the hovel he had shared with his family all his life.

Yesternight I slept in the woods among the moldered corpses of heroes and invaders. And only the night before, with my family. So close is my village, almost a near neighbor of Mitherhome. Yet except for the soldiers who went away to the wars, which man of Farzibeck has traveled as far as me, or learned as much as I've already learned?

He could hear Father's voice answering him. "Learn? You've learned nothing, except how to be a slave in a fool's house, where a southerman lords it over you and a girl mocks you and you will grow nothing in the earth, only carry water and pour water, and chop vegetables for others to eat."

"Shut up," he said to his father.

How many times had he thought it, but dared not say the words? He had been slapped and shoved and punched and kicked a hundred times or more, as if he *had* spoken with such insolence. It was about time he finally said the things that he had already been punished for. He could swear at his Father every day for a year and not be caught up with what the man owed him.

And as he went to sleep, he thought of Lark, so prudish, but so generous; so angry, but such a good storyteller. She talks to the birds and the birds obey her, yet she doesn't think that she's a birdfriend; what could a birdfriend do more than she did, keeping the birds away from the house because she could not serve them well here? A strange world, where someone could be a mage and yet deny it so thoroughly that she did not believe in her own power and therefore could never use it.

It would be wonderful to be a birdfriend, for it was said that beastmages could choose a clant, an animal that was like a second self to them. And having chosen a clant, they could learn to put their soul inside the creature, and see through its eyes, and feel all that it felt, and hear all that it heard. A birdfriend could use her clant to spy on people, or just to soar above the earth, or perhaps to take a hare or rabbit and bring it home, if the bird was a raptor. A birdmage would never have to starve.

But since Lark did not think she was a mage, she would have no clant, and thus would never fly or hunt or spy, but just do laundry and keep the birds away more thoroughly than any scarecrow.

If I were a beastmage I would ride with my clant every night while my own body slept. I would come to think of my waking hours as a dream, and my sleeping hours as my true life, soaring through clouds or, as a lion or wolf, stalking through the forest or grassland, free and strong and fearless.

With my luck, though, I'd be a mousemage, and spend my clant-hours fleeing from every predator.

He slept and dreamed himself a mouse living inside the walls of the kitchen, scampering out in the darkness to steal food.

And all the night, his palm pressed against the wall of the hearthroot stones, and he could feel the earth beneath, all the deep stone of it, cool and hard near the surface of the earth, but hotter and softer as you went deep, until it flowed like honey, a vast sweet fiery ocean of molten rock a thousand times more voluminous and ten thousand times heavier than the sea. It felt to him as if it were his own blood, and his heart pumped it.

The awkwardness of the first day soon faded. Each day Runnel arose before dawn and went to the fountain before most of the women of Hetterferry were up. There he filled the jar and carried it back, returned and filled it again, and then again—enough water for most days' work. There were even days when he made only two trips, because the cistern was full.

At first Lark was grateful, for this was her heaviest duty, and since she filled the jar only half full, she used to take six trips. But after days and weeks of it, she simply took it for granted—as Runnel had meant that she should. Let her work at tasks that required the skill of her clever hands. Runnel had no great skill. The best he achieved was adequacy—but at most household tasks, that was enough.

He continued in the kitchen, because Nikwiz and Sourwell were good and patient teachers. He soon abandoned their expensive metal knives and used the chipped obsidian that everyone used in Farzibeck. The knives were constantly dulled on the cutting stones and had to be sharpened, but the obsidian never seemed to lose its edge, and it fit into his hand more comfortably than any metal blade, however well-wrapped in leather the hilt might be.

Lark and he became friends, but not eager ones. When

they were together on a task, they worked harmoniously, and even bantered together in a comfortable way. But whole days would go by in which they did not see each other, since Lark's work was mostly indoors, now that Runnel was doing most of the outdoor tasks. Only the laundry brought her out, and Runnel found himself looking forward to laundry days, not because he had any particular yearning for her, but because compared to the perfect dance between Nikwiz and Sourwell, which shut out all others, her company was the best to be had in the stonemage's house.

Every week or so, there would be visitors who stayed for a night or two and then went on. Many of them were traders and merchants, and Lord Brickel would dine with them and then keep them company as they went out into the Hetterferry market to trade with the downriver, crossriver, and landbound merchants.

Runnel soon learned that Lord Brickel never did stonework of any kind, not for sale and not for gifts—the Mithermages paid him to work only for them, so that between tasks he was idle. Demwor was ever vigilant.

And yet, when Runnel went down into the cellar during the master's dinners with his visitors, he was press against the hearthroot stones and hear snatches of their conversations, for the stone carried sound that wooden doors and floors hid from hearing. Though the conversations were never clear, he began to realize that their language was guarded. Their laughter was out of proportion to things that were said; answers made no sense in relation to their questions. There must be double meanings hidden in their words.

Why, in the home of the stonemage of Mitherhome, would visitors speak with veiled intent? It occurred to him that these merchants and traders were also worshippers of Tewstan. Perhaps some of them were stonemages themselves.

Runnel's curiosity would not leave him alone. What were they saying? More to the point: What *weren't* they saying?

If only Demwor were not always in and out of the great hall: conversations never took an interesting turn when he was there. Not that Demwor's spying was inappropriate—perhaps there was some conspiracy of stonemages. But Demwor would never hear of it, not the way he was going about it. Nor would Runnel ever hear the conversation of mages.

The only hope of it was to get Demwor out of the great hall. And Demwor would never stop spying…unless he had another spy.

Runnel began to find excuses to be in the kitchen during dinner, and then took any excuse to carry this and that into the great hall. This way he could see the visitors, even though he heard less than he did when he listened in the cellar. Gradually, he transformed his own role until he waited in the room throughout the meal, ready to carry messages, run errands, or carry away finished bowls and platters. He remained absolutely silent, except when he had to deliver a message from the kitchen.

At first Demwor seemed irritated with him, until Runnel came to him one morning and began to ask him about the things Lord Brickel's visitors had spoken of the night before. In the process of asking him questions, Runnel made it obvious that he had memorized most of the conversation—and his questions were about the very things that seemed to be hinting at stonemagery. "Come to me any time with your questions," said Demwor.

So Runnel was now welcomed in the great hall—by Demwor, anyway. The more Runnel was able to repeat the conversations of the night before, the more Demwor left him alone in the room with Lord Brickel and his guests.

Runnel's weekly coin was doubled.

He felt guilty for his double betrayal. For he was, indeed, spying on Lord Brickel. But he wasn't spying as well as Demwor wanted. He always reported the kinds of things Demwor himself used to hear. But he never reported when Lord Brickel and his visitors slipped and revealed more than they meant to. So he was taking Demwor's coin under false pretenses.

As Demwor began to let Runnel do all his listening, Runnel would catch Lord Brickel gazing at him now and then, studying him. Each time Runnel tucked his head into a properly servile position, hiding the arrogant expression that he now knew his face always bore. Runnel assumed that Lord Brickel knew he was Demwor's spy; he also guessed that Brickel was pondering just how stupid Runnel might be, and how much could be said in front of him.

Gradually, as Runnel's reports to Demwor omitted anything unusually incriminating, Lord Brickel grew more candid with his guests. They would glance at Runnel, but Lord Brickel would only smile. He could never speak aloud about Runnel's new role as ineffective spy, in case Runnel was not an ally but merely obtuse; still, it was clear to the guests that Lord Brickel did not regard him as much of a danger.

As high summer came, the visitors became more common, sometimes two or three in a week, and sometimes overlapping their visits. Meanwhile, Demwor was often out at night, pursuing his own business, relying on Runnel's report the next morning to tell him what was said in the great hall.

One of the guests was a dealer in marble named Stokhos, and it was plain he was important—the other two visitors and

Lord Brickel himself attended to his every word, and he was full of inscrutable sayings that must be codes that only stonemages could understand. If Demwor had been in the room, the very meaninglessness of their conversation would have made him suspicious, and Lord Brickel's interview with him the next day would have been difficult. Runnel would report none of the oddities. But he would remember them, and try to make sense of them later.

In the midst of the conversation, Stokhos arose from the table to piss into the fireplace; with Demwor gone, they all did this, as if it were some kind of offering to the stone, or perhaps just marking themselves as belonging here, like dogs that peed their way around the fields and fences of Farzibeck. But when Stokhos rested his bare hand against the hearthstone, he suddenly stopped, dropped his tunic back down to cover himself, and turned to face the others.

"When did this come to life?" he asked.

The words were too plain, and Lord Brickel glanced at Runnel nervously. Runnel tucked his chin and looked at the floor.

Footsteps told him that the guests were all going to the hearth and touching it.

"Alive all the way down to the heart," said Stokhos. "I didn't think you had it in you, friend."

They called Lord Brickel "friend," and Runnel had long since guessed that by this they were giving him his title cobblefriend, the lowest degree of stonemage—but still a true mage, and not just a worshipper of Tewstan.

"Currents hide under still water, brother," said Brickel, who alone seemed not to have risen from the table. The title "brother" implied that Stokhos was a rockbrother, the middle degree of stonemage.

"So you do your work under the very gaze of the birds of heaven?" asked Stokhos—which, Runnel guessed, meant, You practice stonemagery here in the house with Demwor watching?

"The nest is twigs, but the bird still builds it in a sturdy tree." To Runnel, that meant: I have to live in a wooden house, but that doesn't mean the stone parts can't be connected to the deepest living rock.

The trouble was that Runnel knew the hearth was not alive. Or at least it hadn't been. It *touched* the earth, with no wood under it like the flagstones of the cellar floor. Small stones linked it to bedrock. But Stokhos was saying that it was living rock—all of one piece.

"Clever," said one of the other guests. "It all looks loose from the surface, but yes, it *is* all of one piece, deep inside."

"Subtle," said another. The admiration in their voices was obvious.

"You were never that good a student in school," said Stokhos, chuckling—but the chuckle was artificial. He was genuinely surprised.

"A man never stops learning," said Lord Brickel.

"But a wise man does not show his enemies what he has learned," said Stokhos. Runnel understood: You risk being discovered.

"The fish sees only what's in the water," said Lord Brickel. Meaning: The watermages of Mitherhome can't tell what's going on deep inside the stone.

"But when the spring flood rolls loose cobbles down the stream, the fish sees *that*." Meaning: What if they tried to repair or remove some of this stone, and found it was no longer loose?

"Living stone doesn't roll with the flood," said Lord Brickel. Meaning: Why would anyone repair this hearth when living rock will never need repairing?

"Well," said Stokhos, resuming his seat. "A bird like me can tell if the tree is sound before building his nest—but such as I cannot heal a dead tree and bring it back to life."

Did that mean that Lord Brickel had leapt past the level of a rockbrother to do work that only stonefathers could do? No wonder Stokhos sounded surprised. A true stonefather was rare; a fathermage was rare in any of the houses of magic. That's why in Lark's story of the great battle with the Verylludden, the stonemages had been only cobblefriends and rockbrothers, and had to work together to do what a stonefather could have done alone. There might not have been a stonefather in all the world, or not one close enough to get to Mitherhome in time to save it.

From things he had heard all his life, he had always believed that magery was a combination of what you were born with, what you learned, and what you earned. The stories of wolf-mages that alternately terrified and fascinated the children of Farzibeck talked of how a child would find that dogs were always drawn to him, and then his parents would fear he might be a wolfmage, and kept him away from dogs. In the stories, the child always found a wolfpup out in the forest and fed and protected it, and thus gained in power among the wolves, not just because of his inborn ability, but also because he took risks and spent many hours serving and saving a wolfkin. But the stories all implied that a mage could never surpass the level of ability born in him.

Even if greater power could be earned, how could Lord Brickel have earned it when he was expressly forbidden to serve the stone? Of course, under that circumstance, it might be that any small service he gave could be magnified by the risk. That must be it.

What surprised Runnel most, however, had nothing to do with Lord Brickel. It was when Stokhos said, "A bird like me can tell if the tree is sound." To Runnel, this clearly meant that only a rockbrother could sense whether stone was living or not.

But *I* can do that.

The idea of this took his breath away. He was like the wolfmages in the stories. He was like *Lark*—having a mage's power without realizing it. He had thought that at most he might be a pebbleson, a person who liked stone but had no power over it. After all, wasn't he a worshipper of Yeggut, like all his village?

And how had he ever served stone. How *could* you serve stone, except to bring it back to life when it was dead? And since that was a thing that only a stonefather could do, how could stonemages earn any increase in power? Yet Lord Brickel had done it.

Then it dawned on him. If he was indeed a rockbrother, or at least had one of the powers of a rockbrother, then when he came to this house, perhaps the power of two stonemages—one trained and one raw and untrained—combined so that the trained one, Lord Brickel, could do things beyond his ability alone.

I'm serving here in ways that I hadn't even guessed, thought Runnel. It made him proud to be useful, not just in the housework, but in the magery itself.

The meal went on, but the conversation shifted to safer subjects—or else the code was more obscure and Runnel didn't know how to understand it. No matter—they began to send him out for more ale and finally for a second round of food, which he knew would irritate Sourwell, though Nikwiz never seemed to mind. It was a late night, and when Demwor came home and saw the dinner was still going on, he sent Runnel to bed. "I'll tend them myself till they finally notice it's late," said the steward. "I'll tell the master myself if I have to—he has much work to do tomorrow."

"Can I go along?" asked Runnel.

"Ebb will be glad of the help in carrying the master's touchstones." It was the first Runnel had heard of "touchstones," so he was all the more eager for morning. He would learn something about what stonemages actually *do*—he had only realized his own magery just in time to realize that he could profit from the learning.

As always, Runnel "went to bed" by climbing up to his attic room and sitting in the middle of the floor, practicing controlling his dread of being so far from stone. Tonight he managed it easily, for now he understood why he needed the stone so much, and why he feared being in structures that to other people felt safe and solid. Here he would wait until the house was fully quiet, and then creep down to the cellar to sleep. It never mattered to him that he got less sleep than anyone. As long as he could sleep with his hand touching the stone of the hearthroot, then he could get his full rest in only a few hours, and awaken refreshed long before light. But if he slept away from stone, then his rest was fitful waking often, and in the morning he felt as though he hadn't slept at all.

Because I'm a stonemage!

He wondered how Lord Brickel managed to sleep. There was no channel of stone from *his* bedroom down to the earth.

The master slept on a wooden bed, which rested on a wooden floor, which rested on wooden beams and joists.

Runnel lay down on the attic floor and closed his eyes as he listened for the sounds of the house to quiet down.

He awoke in darkness and silence.

The floor trembled under him. He sprang to his feet. How had he slept? That had never been possible before on this high wooden floor. But maybe he could do it, now that he knew why he feared being away from stone.

The things he had learned tonight flooded back into his mind. He felt ridiculous.

I was even more blind than Lark, he thought. She knew she *might* be a mage, and refused to believe it. It never even crossed my mind about myself.

He was hungry to get down to the cellar and feel what Stokhos had felt in the hearthstones. Lord Brickel must have bonded the stones into a living whole during the day yesterday, or surely Runnel would have felt the change the night before. It must have been a great undertaking.

But Lord Brickel had been out at the dock of Hetterferry most of the day, keeping company with his visitors and greeting Stokhos, who only arrived that afternoon. How could he have done it in the few hours he spent at home?

Because he was so excited, Runnel found himself being careless and making a bit of noise on the stairs. That was no problem on the way down to the main floor—he could always say he was going out to pee. But then he really *would* have to do it, and put off going down to the cellar till later. Better not to waken anyone. So he was extra careful going down the rest of the stairs.

There were still a couple of candles guttering on their sconces on the main floor, but they were nearly gone. To his surprise, going down the cellar steps, there was a light ahead of him. Someone was down there, but by now his feet were visible. He had been seen. So there was nothing for it but to continue, and decide what lie to tell based on who was down there. If it was Demwor, he could tell him that he was looking for him to report to him now, since they'd be busy in the morning.

It was Lord Brickel himself, holding a candle and pressing the other hand on the hearthroot stones. As soon as he recognized Runnel in the dim light, he set down the candle and beckoned.

When Runnel was close enough that they could talk in whispers, Brickel took him by the shoulder and brought his lips close to Runnel's ears.

"What are you doing to me?" he asked.

Runnel thought he was asking about the things he told to Demwor. "I never tell him anything that you didn't used to say in front of him."

The hand squeezed harder. "Where did you study?"

Now Runnel was confused. "I never studied anything, sir."

"To do this—I tried to dislodge a stone down here, any of them, an easy thing. Dislodge it, pull it out, push it back in, it's what I do. Only I can't. The stones are all of a piece. They're alive, as Stokhos said. And don't pretend you don't know what I'm talking about. I know you understand us. I *trusted* you."

No point in pretending now. "It wasn't alive when I first came down here," said Runnel.

"So you can tell which stones are living and which are dead?"

"I didn't know that it was magery," said Runnel. "Nobody told me."

"You can't be that stupid."

Runnel grew angry. "I grew up in a village that's faithful to Yeggut. Who would teach me anything about stone?"

"It's not just the hearthstones, it's the flagstones, too. They underlay the floor with wood, but you bound all the stones together into a continuous sheet of living stone. Do you think they won't be able to tell? All he has to do is *walk* down here and feel how they don't spring back up under his feet."

"He" had to mean Demwor. "He sends me down here," said Brickel.

"But one day he won't. You'll be on another errand, and he'll come down himself, and he'll realize what you've done. Only he'll think *I* bound them together, and I'll lose my position. And if he realizes that it's *living* rock, I'll lose my life."

"But *didn't* you do it?" Runnel reached for the hearthstones and then shook his head. "My lord, these hearthstones are no different from the way they were when I got up this morning. I mean yesterday morning."

"Why would you have checked them yesterday if you didn't know something was changing with them?"

"I didn't *check* them," said Runnel. "I sleep down here."

"So you can't tell if these stones are living rock?"

Runnel pressed his hand against the stone and deliberately traced the stone inside, to find where it ended...and it didn't. It kept going down into the earth, in a single column. It never rested on hard-packed earth. All the tiny stones that had once formed a thousand chains down to bedrock were now a single great sweep of stone that grew out of the bedrock and soared through soil till it came out here as hearthstones and flagstone, creased where they had once been separate pieces, but now fused inside, where it was hidden from view.

"I didn't...I didn't *look*," said Runnel. "I never noticed a difference, it felt the same every day."

"You've been sleeping down here?" asked Lord Brickel. "Show me."

Runnel lay down where he always did, and pressed his hand against the stone.

"Aw, Tewstan, what a fool," said Brickel. "A natural mage sleeps every night with his hands in the stone."

"Not *in* the stone, my lord," said Runnel.

"Of course your hand is in the stone, and the stone is in your hand. You've been pouring your life into the stone, and the stone has been pouring strength into your body. Look at your face; I should have seen it, it's half stone already."

Runnel touched his hand to his face. It felt like ordinary flesh to him.

"And Demwor tells me you can carry full water jars without ever stopping to rest, and I don't even *wonder*? I deserve whatever happens to me."

"Why should anything happen to you, my lord?" asked Runnel.

"Because I swore an oath that I was nothing but a cobblefriend, and by Tewstan it was the truth. But they'll never believe that it's sheer chance that brought a...a *stonefather* here to my house."

"A what?" A thrill went through Runnel. He wasn't sure if it was fear or joy. Both, probably.

"What do you think, that cobblefriends and rockbrothers can do this? You slept your way through the stone—of course it joined to the bedrock, to the whole globe of living rock on which the oceans and the continents float. You're ignorant, you know absolutely nothing, that much is obvious, but you have power. The stone loves you. Don't you see it? Hasn't it shown you its love all your life?"

Runnel thought back to his rock-climbing and realized: The reason I could find cracks and handholds and toeholds where others couldn't was because the stone opened up for me. Because it loved me.

And I love the stone. Like the child wolfmage in the story loves the wolfpup. All my life, I've loved the feel of it in my hand. I've worked with it, built with it, cut with it, climbed it, slept on it when I could. And it never occurred to me that this made me a stonemage.

"It has," he said to Lord Brickel. "But I didn't realize. It was part of being alive, to hold the stone, to climb it."

"And you didn't feel yourself connect with the stone below?"

"I thought it was my dream."

"If you had gone to school in Cyllythu, you'd know. Dreams like that must be told to a master. You would have been known for what you are."

"I can't be a stonefather," said Runnel. "I'm...Runnel."

"Well, you're *not* a stonefather. You have the power of one, but you have no skills at all. You don't even know what you're doing. You can't control it. You can't keep yourself from doing it."

"Teach me."

"Impossible. Not here. Don't you think Demwor would notice? No, you're getting out of here, while I try to take these stones apart one by one."

The thought of dividing the rocks again struck Runnel like a blow. "But...it's alive now."

"It shouldn't be. It *wasn't* till you meddled."

Now he registered what Lord Brickel had said before. "Where will I go?"

"To Cyllythu, of course. Go to the temple of Tewstan and tell them what happened here. Stokhos will vouch for the truth of it, and they'll test you and you'll be fine, I promise. But you're getting out of here tonight."

"I don't know the way. And the soldiers of the guard will challenge me."

"They won't see you. Don't you understand? Just press yourself against the stone walls of the fortress and they'll never see you."

"I've never —"

"I don't have time to argue. You are getting out of here tonight."

"Why can't I wait for day?"

"Because if Demwor challenges me, I will betray you, do you understand? It's the only way to keep him from thinking *I* did all this. So yes, I'll tell him the truth about you—that you clearly didn't know what you were doing, that it was an accident. But do you think they'll care? A stonefather, here in Hetterferry, at the very base of the Mitherjut."

"What will they do?" asked Runnel.

"What they do to stonemages: Drown you, then burn your body to ash and stir it into the living water."

"And you'd let them do that to *me*, just so you don't lose your job?"

"Stupid boy, it's not *my* job. It's the only connection the stonefolk still have with the Mitherjut. Even if they don't kill me, they'll never let another stonemage into this whole valley. My only hope of keeping trust is to denounce you myself. Now get out of here, out of the house, out of the garden, onto the street, while I take apart the mess you've made down here."

The "mess" was living stone, and it made Runnel sick at heart to think of it.

"I can't go," he said. "I can't let you do it."

"What?" demanded Lord Brickel.

"I can't let you kill the stone."

"And yet you will," said Lord Brickel.

Brickel laid his hand on a stone and Runnel could feel what he was doing—feel the cracks growing where they had originally been, the stones separating. Dying.

And without even trying to, Runnel flowed the stone back together again.

"Tewstan!" whispered Brickel. "I said get out."

"And leave the stones to die?"

"Stop being such a child," said Lord Brickel. "These stones would gladly die, for the sake of the stonemages someday returning to Mitherjut. I'm not *killing* them, I'm helping them make their sacrifice. Now go, upstairs, out. We've talked for far too long."

Runnel tried to make sense of it all. He could feel the death of the stones under Brickel's hand; yet he could also understand that it might be necessary. Didn't cobblefriends work with dead stone all the time? Weren't streets cobbled with it? And didn't those dead stones feel warm and good under Runnel's feet? Dead wasn't *dead,* not the way people died. A stone could be cut off, but it could then be put back and joined again to the living rock, and it would live again itself. He must let this happen.

I'm a stonefather. I must do what's good for all the stone, the way the packfather in the story willingly died in his clantbody to save the pack.

He went to the stairs and climbed to the main floor. He owned nothing; there was nothing to take with him but the clothes he wore. And maybe a single obsidian from the kitchen.

Runnel walked quietly across the floor to the back door that led out to the kitchen. When he opened the door, Demwor was standing there.

"What are you doing up?" asked Demwor.

"Had to pee," said Runnel.

"Where were you?"

"Asleep," said Runnel.

"I went to the attic. You weren't there. I came out looking to see if you were peeing. I wanted to talk to you about last night. About our *guests.*"

"I *am* peeing."

"Where were you when I looked in the attic?"

Where could he claim to have been that would put him inside the house now, still needing to urinate?

Runnel raised his voice a little louder as he stepped out onto the stone steps leading down into the garden. "Lord Brickel wanted to talk to me about tomorrow's work," he said.

He pressed his feet into the stone and felt the connection of living rock all the way to the hearthroot where Lord Brickel was working. He found a section that was still alive and pushed it, squeezed it out so it bulged. Surely Lord Brickel would see it and realize it was a warning.

"He wanted to take me instead of Ebb," said Runnel, loudly enough that if Lord Brickel would just come up from the cellar, he'd hear. "To work in the city."

"You *asked* him, didn't you?" said Demwor.

"Why would I, sir?" asked Runnel. "You already told me I'd bear half the burden of touchstones."

Demwor glowered. "Why would he want to *talk* to you about it? You'll do what you're told."

"He doesn't know me that well, but I'm…well, quicker than Ebb. Or at least he wanted to make sure of it. Maybe there are things he needs that Ebb has never been able to do. I don't know, sir. I just do what I'm told."

"What did they talk about last night?" demanded Demwor.

Suddenly Lord Brickel was in the doorway behind Runnel. "What did you just ask my servant?"

Demwor clamped his mouth shut.

"Are you spying on me, Demwor?"

What, thought Runnel, was that a secret? No, it was a pretense that he was just a steward. Now the pretense is broken.

"Is this how the Mithermages treat me? Have I not performed every service, and kept faith with every term of our agreement?"

"You have these visitors," said Demwor.

"I'm allowed to have friends come to see me," said Lord Brickel. "It's in the terms."

While they talked, Runnel was continuing Lord Brickel's work, separating the stones in the hearth, in the hearthroot, on the cellar floor. He did it more quickly than Lord Brickel had, and he didn't have to be touching the very stone he was working on. An hour ago he wouldn't even have known to try what he was doing, but having seen Lord Brickel do it he now knew what it felt like, and how to show the stone, how to flow through it and make the separation.

And Lord Brickel was right. The stone did not groan; it accepted the separation. It knew that Runnel was doing right, protecting it by this separation. It had loved him for joining them together, but it did not hate him for separating them now.

"You're not allowed to bring stonemages here," said Demwor.

"Exactly," said Lord Brickel. "But who do you think my friends *are*? All pebblesons, at least, worshippers of Tewstan."

"A worship that's forbidden here."

"And we don't *worship* here," said Lord Brickel patiently. "But you know that just as puddlesons have a bit of power clinging to them because of their service to Yeggut, so do pebblesons because of their service to Tewstan. If you've detected some sort of power in them, that's why. But no *mages*."

"I've seen the links between you and them," said Demwor.

So he was key—not really a mage, but able to find magical links.

"Of course," said Lord Brickel. "But never when I'm working. I do no magery for the city when such links are present. If you're what I think you are, then you know that. You *know* I've never bound myself to stone except when the Mithermages ask me to."

Runnel realized that was a warning. If Demwor really *was* a key, he would sense Runnel's connection to the stone beneath his feet the moment he looked for it. So he stepped back up over the wooden sill and onto the wooden floor, and held the wooden doorframe.

In case Lord Brickel had not heard what he said earlier, Runnel chimed in. "I *told* you he wanted to speak to me about what we'd do tomorrow," he said. "Now can I go pee?"

"What *will* you do tomorrow?" Demwor asked Lord Brickel.

"My duty," said Lord Brickel. "As of this moment you are not my steward. If you stay here, then it's as a spy, and as long as they have a spy with me, they're in breach of the contract."

As Runnel headed into the bushes where he routinely peed—he saved the private house for other uses—he could still hear the argument.

"Well, then, you know I was using the boy as a spy," said Demwor. "So is he going as well?"

"If you aren't here to ask him, whom will he tell? He works hard and he's ignorant. *You're* the one who's leaving. Now. We'll put your things out the front gate in the morning."

"Where am I supposed to go at this time of the morning?" asked Demwor.

"To your masters, to report on me," said Lord Brickel. "Tell them that their bridges and arches can all fall down, now that I know I've been serving oathbreakers."

"You knew I was a spy."

"I wondered," said Lord Brickel. "*Now* I know. Get out."

What have I done? thought Runnel. I never meant for any of this to happen.

When he got back to the house, Lord Brickel and Demwor were both gone—presumably to the gate.

Runnel ran down into the cellar and quickly finished the work of separating the stones. He tried not to think of it as killing them. Someday I'll make you whole again, he thought over and over, promising Tewstan, the stone god.

If you think of it as stone, how can you talk to it? But if it's Tewstan, a god, then you can pray, and hope to be heard.

Yet he felt a twinge of guilt, for he had grown up with the worship of Yeggut, the god of water, the master of all things, who brings life to the desert and tears down mountains.

How did I become a stonemage, when all my thought was of Yeggut?

It is not the rituals of worship that please the gods, he

realized. I worshipped Yeggut, but I climbed the stone, I put my fingers into the rock. There in the mountains, it was the stone heart of the world that made me who I am, no matter who or what I prayed to.

THE WETWIZARDS OF Mitherhome came for Brickel when the sun was halfway to noon. The day was cool and bright, so many of the people of Hetterferry came out to watch the procession. Lord Brickel wore an elaborate costume that Runnel thought looked ridiculous, but it seemed to impress everyone else. What does clothing have to do with magery? But the watermages were also in fancy headdresses and bright-colored robes, and there were boys carrying banners and pipes and drums being played as they walked down to the dock.

There was a raft there waiting for them. It reminded Runnel of the raft he had once helped to load, his first day in Hetterferry. If the raft had carried him to Mitherhome that day, would he ever have discovered his ability? Then again, if he had never discovered his power, would he be more or less happy?

Of course, as far as anyone knew he was only the stonemage's boy, carrying on his back a heavy load of many different kinds of rock—small samples of each, but in the aggregate, it felt like he was carrying a wall. Yet he *could* carry it, and he wondered if it was because the stone was somehow lighter for him than for other people. Or perhaps there was enough stone in *him* that he was sturdier and could bear more of a burden. That would explain why he could carry a full waterjar, even though he was not a full-grown man. Maybe everything about him that mattered came back to the stone in his heart.

They were poled across the water to Mitherhome, and then began the long trek up the endless stairways to the upper level of the city. Their course wound around the steep slopes of Mitherjut, and as Runnel's bare feet trod the stone steps he could feel a throbbing inside the mountain, not like a heartbeat, but rather like the slow fluttering of a huge bird that was trapped and could not get free. He thought of trying to find the source of it, but Lord Brickel had warned him to do nothing, seek nothing, *think* nothing about stone. "It's too dangerous," said Brickel. "Look what you did to the stones of this house—in your sleep, without even meaning to."

So Runnel did not explore the stone. Instead he trod the steps upward, upward, with the well-maintained city wall on one hand and the buildings clinging to the steep slope on the other.

They came to a gate in the wall and went through it. In only a few steps they were at the brink of a cliff—not the steep drop-off of the Stonemages' Ditch that he had seen on his first day, but a natural channel cut by water. A stone bridge with a single arch led across the water. It was this bridge that Lord Brickel had been brought to strengthen. And without even trying to, Runnel could see why. All the vibration of carts and pedestrians crossing the bridge had vibrated the stones, making them rub against each other, shrinking them. The arch was sagging, putting outward pressure on the stones near the edges. They were going to break free, and the whole bridge would come down as the loss of a few stones weakened the rest. Maybe in a year. Maybe in a month. But the bridge was not strong.

Lord Brickel walked out onto the bridge and knelt, then lay on it, face down, as if he were staring into the stone. Runnel stood by him, the bag at the ready. Brickel raised a hand from the surface, and Runnel brought the mouth of the bag to his hand. Brickel rummaged through it and came out with a cobble of granite and another of quartz. These he now held in each hand and pressed them into the stone.

He's not doing a thing, thought Runnel. This bridge is failing, and he's doing nothing but making a show. It's fakery.

When it falls, people will die.

But if Runnel fused a few of the stones together, right in the center of the bridge, so they were one piece, no one could see from the outside, but the stones would no longer rub against each other, and the pressures would return to being vertical instead of horizontal, as the bridge was designed. As long as he was careful not to let the fusing go right to the living rock at the ends of the bridge, the stone would not come to life.

It was so simple, so subtle, to link stone to stone.

But it got away from him. Runnel hadn't the skill or self-control to stop himself in time. The fusing went beyond his intention. The bridge linked to the living stone at both ends of the bridge.

Lord Brickel raised himself up on his elbows and cried out, "No!"

Underneath the bridge, the water suddenly roiled and splashed, as if it were angry.

"What have you done!" cried one of the watermages.

"He's tunneled the stream!" shouted another.

At once they reached down and dragged Brickel to his feet. One of them made as if to drag him to the edge of the bridge and cast him off, but the others held firm and did not let him do it.

"You're no cobblefriend!" said the leader of the watermages. "You roofed the stream with living rock! You made

a tunnel of it! Sacrilege! All along you've lied to us. You're a stonefather!"

Lord Brickel looked long into Runnel's eyes. But he did not say, It wasn't me, it was this boy. He said nothing at all as they dragged him from the bridge, back through the gate, and on up the stairs into the city.

Runnel followed, carrying the bag of stones, cursing himself for a fool. It did not help Lord Brickel that Runnel had made the fatal error by accident. Nor was it an excuse that he did not know that water hates to be roofed and tunneled, that it constantly struggles to break free. And how, above all, could he have known that the watermages would sense the moment the bridge became living rock?

It would do no good to declare himself to be the stonefather, Runnel knew. For then Lord Brickel would be charged with knowingly allowing another stonemage to practice in the city, and the penalty would be the same. They would both be punished then.

I have to free him, thought Runnel. I did this to him by disobeying him. It's my responsibility now to get him out of it.

Runnel followed until they came into the main city, which clung to the southwest shore of the Mitherlough. Most of the city was outside of the walls, which ran much higher up the slope of Mitherjut. They took Lord Brickel to a single tower that stood at the far point of a stubby peninsula that projected into the lake. When Runnel tried to follow them inside, one of the watermages stopped him.

"I belong with my master," said Runnel.

"Where he's going, you don't wish to go," said the watermage.

"What will you do to him?"

"What he agreed to by the contract he signed when he first came here," said the watermage. "He knew the penalty."

Runnel wanted to shout that Lord Brickel was *not* a stonefather, that he had only discovered Runnel's abilities last night, that there was no way he could have known or prevented Runnel's foolishness. I'll undo it, Runnel wanted to say, I'll make it back the way it was. But that would accomplish nothing—except to get Runnel inside the tower, subject to the same penalty that Lord Brickel was now facing.

He thought of going back to the stonemage's house and asking Lark's advice. But what would that accomplish, except to take him farther from Lord Brickel? Lark wouldn't know what a stonefather could do, or ought to do.

He thought back to her story of the stonemages in the great war. What had she said? "They bared again the rocks of the holy place, and lay naked upon the stone, and the rockbrothers sank into it as the cobblefriends sang." He had no cobblefriends to sing for him, nor did he have any notion what their songs might have been. But he was a stonefather—if the rockbrothers could sink into the rock, so could he. Sink into the rock of the tower wall, and come out the other side—the inside, where Lord Brickel is held. I can bring him out again the same way, or tear open a door if I want to.

He walked around the tower to a spot that was not observed and pressed his hands against the stone. But this was not living rock. He could climb it, and gaps would open for his fingers and toes, but he could not merge with it, as he could with living rock.

Just as well that he had failed, for as he leaned against the wall, someone walked around the tower into view. Demwor.

"I wondered where you'd got to," said the former steward. "See what your fool of a master has done now?"

"I don't know what he did," said Runnel.

"He revealed himself," said Demwor. "And he'll die for it. Now come with me—I'm to dispose of all the stonemage's property."

"I'm not his property," said Runnel. "I'm a free man."

"Man?" said Demwor. "You're a boy, and barely that. But a free one? That's your choice. A *free* boy will have nothing to eat and nowhere to sleep. You can eat the stones in that bag, for all I care. Come with me now, and you still have a place; stay here, and I'll have you ejected from the city under the vagabond laws, for you have no place here, neither a master nor kin." Demwor reached to take Runnel by the shoulder.

Runnel dodged away, then reached into the bag and pulled out a cobble of sandstone. "Don't make me throw this at your head," said Runnel. "I don't miss."

"Are you threatening a citizen?"

"I'm protecting myself from a man who wants to lay hands on me," said Runnel.

Demwor backed off one step. "Is that how you'll have it, then? Fine. When I return, it'll be with soldiers, and you'll be ejected from the city by *them*. I don't have to lay a hand on you."

As soon as Demwor walked away, Runnel dropped the bag and began to run. Back the way he had come, till he was through the walls and up to the highest point of the road that led around Mitherjut. But instead of continuing down to where the bridge was, Runnel scrambled up the steep slope, away from the road, up toward the peak.

It might not have been the smartest move. For he soon discovered that near the peak, a spring gave birth to a stream, and it must have been a place very holy to Yeggut, because the stream was lined with the huts of sacred hermits, who would come out several times a day and immerse themselves in the stream, letting it flow over them until they were so cold they could barely move. And around the spring there were the houses of priests, and several temples, and a constant stream of visitors coming and going.

But it was the very peak that Runnel wanted, not the spring or the stream. And at the peak, there was just the ruined stone circle that had once been a dome of living rock, in Lark's story. Here it was that the bodies of the stonemages were burned alive inside that stone oven, as their payment for saving the city. A place of treachery. Mitherhome had first been built by stonemages; the watermages dispossessed them and ruled over them, and then, when the stonemages might have thought they'd earned the right to be brought back into equality in their own city, they were murdered.

There was no one here in these ruins. It was not holy ground, as far as the watermages were concerned.

But it was to Runnel. He could feel the throbbing again here, stronger than ever. I have found the heart of the mountain. Maybe the heart of the world.

Following the words of Lark's story, Runnel took off all his clothes and lay down upon the living rock, right where one of the rockbrothers must have lain, back when the battle was raging, and there was no hope for the city.

The sun shone down on him—it was afternoon now, and despite the coolness of the air, the sun was bakingly warm. Runnel realized, now that he was lying still, that his own body was trembling. What have I done? Brickel told me to do nothing, and I thought I knew better. I thought I was saving a bridge, and instead I've cost him his life.

The throbbing under him grew stronger.

He began to sink into the stone.

I'm not doing this, he thought. I'm not pushing myself into the stone. I'm just lying here, and the stone is welcoming me.

He sank; the stone closed over him. He lay in darkness, but he could still feel the sun beating on his skin. No, not on his skin—on the stone above him. The stone of Mitherjut, that was his skin now. He sank into the stone, but the stone also sank into him. He could feel the whole Mitherjut as if it were part of his body.

And he was not alone.

"Stonefather," came a whisper. It was repeated, again and again, until two dozen at least had called to him.

"Who are you?" he asked. Only he did not move his lips—could not move them. Yet he heard his own voice as if he had spoken aloud.

"You know who we are," said one of them. "We have waited long for you."

"Are you the rockbrothers who created Stonemages' Ditch? The ones who won the battle and then were burned?"

"They burned our bodies," said one of them. And another,

and another. "Our inselves died. But our outselves were wandering in the stone, shaping it. That is all that lives, and we are fading. We have waited for a stonefather to come. Now you are here. Save the city, Stonefather!"

Save the city? What was *that* about? "*You* saved the city," he said. "From the Veryludden."

"Long ago," said the voices. "And they were only men. It is from the flowing stone we save the city. Feel how it wants to rise."

It was as if they led him, for even though his body did not move, he was traveling through the rock. "Is this my outself that you lead through the stone?" he asked them, and they said, "Yes."

They took him down under the Mitherjut to where a thick dome of cold rock pressed down as under it a hot dome of seething, flowing magma pressed upward. "The blood-stone wants to flow. It wants to burst free. We have held it down all these years, but now it grows stronger and we grow weaker. Soon it will break free."

"What can I do?" asked Runnel.

"What we have done. Hold it down. If it breaks free, the Mitherjut will disappear, the city will be utterly destroyed, the lake will become a mere river, and all this good land will be covered in ash and new basalt."

"They killed you. Why don't you let them be destroyed in turn?"

"Mitherstane was built as a partnership of stone and man. What if the watermages rule for this moment? We cannot let the holy city be destroyed."

"I'm supposed to stay here for the rest of my life? Holding down a volcano?"

"Inside the stone your life will be long and longer. Till another stonefather comes."

"I can't. I have to save my master, Lord Brickel."

"He's only a cobblefriend. He can't help in this work."

"You don't understand. It's my fault that he's in trouble. They're going to kill him. I have to set him free from the prison he's in. I have to do it now."

And with that he wrenched himself free from the gentle pressure of their company and began to wander alone through the living stone. It was hard to imagine, deep in the rock, where he was in relation to the city above. Only when he brought his outself near the surface could he feel the cobblestones of the streets and the great buildingstones of the city walls, and the pressure of the heavy buildings as they pressed down into the earth.

He found the tower out on the peninsula and fused the stones of the tower to the bedrock on which they rested, making it a place of living stone. He did not bother to preserve the outward facade of separateness; he knew that the tower would no longer appear to be made of many stones, but of a single, smooth sheet of it, rising straight up out of the earth. Let the watermages see something of his power; let them wonder how it could be happening. He grew stone over the doors of the tower. No watermage could get in or out.

Now that the walls of the tower were alive, his outself could rise up into them, and now, as naturally as if he had been doing it all his life, he formed a body for himself out of the living stone. He gave it eyes, so his outself could see; legs and feets, so it could walk. He pulled his new stone body free of the wall and began to walk the downward spiraling corridor of the tower.

Watermages and guards tried to stop him—they broke their puny weapons on his stone body, and cast their spells, but there was no water in him to obey them, and he brushed them aside and went on.

At the base of the spiral ramp there was a pool of water, at the same level as the lake. Out in the middle of the pool, on a raft of reeds, floated Lord Brickel, tied down, unable to move.

Runnel took his stone body—his clant, for now he knew what he had created—to the edge of the water and knelt. His knees grew into the living rock of the ramp, and drawing on the stone he was once again a part of, he extended his arms, longer, longer, until one of them completely bridged the pool, passing just over the raft on which Brickel was bound. Then with his other hand, he broke open Brickel's bonds.

Brickel climbed onto the bridge the Runnel had formed and walked over the pool to safety. "Runnel," said Brickel. "What good will this do? You should have let them kill me."

Runnel did not know how to make his clant speak. But he pressed his head against Brickel's head, and spoke inside his mind, as he had spoken to the outselves of the rockbrothers. "It's time to undo an old injustice," he said. "Be my voice. It's time for the stonemages to return to Mitherstane."

"That's our dream, but we're not ready."

"You have a stonefather now," said Runnel. "Tell them."

Runnel's clant, his stone body, led the way back up the ramp, to where the wetwizards and soldiers were clustered around what used to be a door.

"Let us out!" they cried. "We won't harm you."

Lord Brickel stepped around Runnel's clant. "Do you think I care about saving myself?" he said. "I bring a message from the Stonefather whose clant you see before you. This is the city of Mitherstane, built by stonemages at the beginning of time. You are the children of treachery, who slew the stonemages who saved you from your enemy. This is the day of reckoning."

"What can we do?" cried the wetwizards.

But then Runnel felt something terrible and strange. The living stone of the tower was being attacked by something that chewed through the stone and turned it into tiny bits of dead dust. A gap opened in the wall, and through it stepped one, then another, then a third creature made of water.

The wetwizards cheered. "The waterfathers bring you your answer, stonefather!"

The three waterclants strode to Runnel's stoneclant and the moment they touched him, he could feel them wearing away the stone of his skin. He tried to replenish himself from the living stone beneath his feet, but there were three of them, and he could not keep up.

So he flowed his clant back down into the living stone of the floor.

Once again, he had left Brickel at the mercy of the watermages.

I was a fool, he thought. I felt all this power, and forgot that the watermages have power of their own. They defeated us before; why did I think that I alone could defeat them now?

"Forget them," murmured the rockbrothers. "Help us suppress the flowing stone."

But Runnel was not going to forget anything. He thought: What can I do to hurt them? How can I make them release Brickel?

He thought of the porous stone in the cistern back at Lord Brickel's house. There, it served as a filter. But here, that kind of stone could serve another purpose entirely.

Runnel sent his outself through the stone that underlay the lake. Starting with a little outcropping of rock surrounded by water, he expanded the stone by making it as porous as the filterstone in the cistern. He expanded it more, with larger holes and channels, and it filled with water. He spread the porousness through more and more of the lake-bed rock, and took it deeper and deeper. As the stone expanded, it rose higher, toward the surface of the lake; the water level fell as the water soaked into the stone.

Until finally there was no lake. Just a single sheet of porous rock, with all the water held inside.

He could feel the flow of the water down the channels as it came to a stop. The water flowing into the lake from the streams and rivers that fed it soaked into the stone as fast as it arrived. There was no lake. Below Mitherjut, there was no river.

Where will you draw your power from now, waterfathers?

He returned to the tower, to the pool in the middle of it, and there, too, he made the stones of the tower porous, so the water was soaked into the floor and walls. The pool was dry. Runnel formed another clant out of the newly-porous stone of the walls and returned up the ramp. The waterclants were no longer there. No one was there.

Where had they taken Brickel?

He emerged from the tower through the hole the waterclants had made. Outside, the streets were deserted. He could see that the sun was low, nearing the horizon—it had taken him longer to swallow up the lake than he had thought.

Where were the people? There were a few, kneeling at what had been the shore—the docks now hung over bare stone. But not the watermages.

Of course, he thought. They've gone to the holy place. To the spring near the peak of Mitherjut.

"It's working," said the rockbrothers. Runnel did not know what they meant—nothing was working.

Runnel's stoneclant strode up the steep, rocky slope and walked directly over the spot where his real body, his inself, lay buried in stone. He could feel his clant tread over him. Then it went down to the spring.

There they held Brickel in the flow of the stream. Brickel was gasping.

The watermages shouted at Runnel's clant. "We'll sacrifice him! We'll drown him if you don't return our water!"

In reply, Runnel turned the streambed porous and soaked up all the water there. The spring ceased to flow.

The watermages wailed.

Brickel rose to his feet. To Runnel's great admiration, Brickel immediately resumed his role as spokesman for the stonefather.

"It is time for you to abide by the ancient treaty," he shouted. "When first the stonemages allowed the waterkin to settle here, you made the vow that stonemages and watermages would dwell in peace here together, in a place holy to us both. You were the ones who broke that vow! You were the ones whose treachery murdered the best of us a hundred years ago! No more will a single cobblefriend live like a prisoner in order to tend the ancient walls and bridges that were built by ancient stonemages. Either we live here together in a place of stone and water, or it remains as it is now, a place where only stone can live."

"We will!" answered the leader of the watermages. "But only if you give back the sacred Mitherlough."

"When you have taken the solemn unbreakable oath in the treaty tower," said Lord Brickel.

"How can we get there from here?" said the watermage. "The Stonemages' Ditch blocks the way."

"Only because you broke down the living bridge we made there."

"It was a tunnel!" said the waterfather.

"It was a bridge!" roared Brickel back at him. "We all know what a tunnel is—it's where your water is now, in millions of tiny tunnels through stone! A bridge that leaves many yards of air between the water and the stone is no tunnel! We will have bridges wherever the stonemages wish to have them. Bridges of living stone that will never break down!"

With that, Runnel began to walk his stoneclant down the dry streambed, and Brickel followed him. When he reached the broken-down wall that had once been the inner defenses of a peninsula, and now marked the edge of the Stonemages' Ditch, Runnel led them along the wall to the place where once a living bridge had cross the canyon—where soldiers had poured over the bridge to slaughter the Veryludden.

While his clant stood on the surface, Runnel himself reached into the living stone and extruded a wide bridge that reached out over the open air and finally met the stone on the other side. Then he walked out onto it with his clant, Lord Brickel following him, and all the watermages after. They walked on through the forest until they reached the tower that Runnel had seen on the first day, when he was trying to find his way into Mitherhome. This was the ancient temple of the treaty, which had long since been converted into a temple of Yeggut.

Runnel reached into the tower and made it, also, a thing of continuous, living stone.

Then he turned and looked out over the sheet of stone where once the little lake had been. To his surprise, he could not see the stone at all. Instead, thick steam rose from the whole surface.

What is happening?

The rockbrothers answered him: "You brought the water down to the flowing stone and cooled it. We are turning it to granite, deeper and deeper, by pouring the heat of the magma into the water."

"I didn't know it would do that."

"The flowing stone is already far below where it used to be. Soon we will need no one to keep it from bursting through. You have saved the holy city."

But at the treaty tower, the watermages saw the steam and wailed. "You're making our holy water vanish!"

"Will the rains not come?" said Brickel. "When the stonefather restores the stone of the lake bed, will the rivers not flow and fill it again? Now in your hot blood and mine, the mixture of water and stone that flows in all of us, we will sign again the treaty that you broke."

The ancient document was sealed under clear quartz; Brickel did not need Runnel's help to separate the quartz from the surrounding stone and lift it off. There he and the watermages opened their veins and dipped pens in blood and signed their names again.

When it was done, Lord Brickel replaced the quartz and fused it again to the granite pedestal.

"Now give us back our lake!" they said.

Runnel first restored the sacred spring and stream that flowed down the slope of Mitherjut. Then he worked his way from the farthest edge of the Mitherlough, shrinking the stone of the lake bed so it was no longer porous. But he did not release the water from the stone; instead, he guided it to flow down to the magma, ever deeper, cooling it more and more. "Yes," murmured the rockbrothers. "It will be as if the stone had never been hot. The flowing stone is deep again, where it belongs."

As the lake bed sank back down, the steam continued to rise. It was not until well after dark that the entire lake bed had been restored. Now the waters of the inflowing rivers flowed out onto the stone, and slowly the lake began to form itself again. It would take many days to refill the lake as it had been. But it would refill.

"Move my household into the city," said Lord Brickel. "We will have a new home in the shadow of Mitherjut, near the walls our ancestors built. I will invite as many stonemages to come to the city as you now have watermages. One for one, our numbers equal. We will sit on your councils in exactly the same numbers as you. We will have an equal voice in the making of the laws. All according to the treaty we have signed today."

And the watermages said yes, for they could see that their lake was coming back to its place.

Runnel flowed his stoneclant into the rock of the treaty tower.

High above, at the crest of the Mitherjut, his body of flesh rose upward out of the stone.

But it was not the same body that had sunk into the stone earlier that day. For he had been too closely bonded with the granite of the mountain, and now his skin was hard and flecked; there was stone in him, all through him. He moved as flexibly as ever, but he could feel that his feet would never grow tired from walking, and only the sharpest obsidian could cut his skin. He was not pure stone like his clant had been, but neither was he pure flesh and bone.

He put on his clothes again and made his way down the way he had come. No one noticed him in the gathering night. He was just a boy walking the streets.

When he got to the low port across from Hetterferry, he only had to tell the ferryman that he was Lord Brickel's servant. After the events of this day, that paid for his passage, for everyone feared the stonemage. After all, they believed that it was Brickel who had done all that was done today. They could not afford to cross him by offending his servant.

At the stonemage's house, Demwor was already there, but his errand had changed. Instead of disposing of the stonemage's wealth, he was supervising the move to the upper city. Runnel immediately began to help with the work, and if anyone noticed that he was now carrying loads far heavier than anything Ebb could bear, they said nothing about it. In the darkness, no one could see how his skin had changed.

All night they worked, carrying everything to the ferry. On the other side, a team of puddlesons lifted everything onto their backs and carried it up the long stair.

By dawn, Lord Brickel's new house was ready, and, exhausted, they all fell into bed and slept well into the next day.

Except for Runnel, who was not weary. He lay down on the stone of the new cellar floor, and fused the stone walls of the house together into living rock. This was the home of a stonefather—it would look like it.

Lord Brickel came to him late in the morning.

"What were you thinking?" he said softly.

"Isn't this what you and your friends were working for?" asked Runnel.

"Were you planning this, then? All of it?"

"None of it," said Runnel. "I didn't have the faintest idea

what I was doing." Then he told Lord Brickel about the rock-brothers, and the near-volcano that the water of the lake had cooled. "I didn't know the water could do that," he said.

"It was Tewstan that guided you," said Brickel.

"Look what it did to me," said Runnel.

He led Brickel up the stairs and stood where the light shone through a window.

Brickel touched his skin. "You are part of the Mitherjut now," he said, in awe. "I've heard of such things, a man taking the stone inside himself. But I've never seen it."

"Will it go away?"

"No," said Brickel. "Not if the lore is true."

"I don't know anything," said Runnel. "Will you take me as your apprentice? Will you teach me?"

"Me? Teach *you*, a stonefather?"

"Is there a stonefather somewhere in the world right now who can do it?"

"No," said Brickel.

"Then what you know, all the lore, all the secrets, I have to learn it. Will you teach me?"

"Of course."

"And let the watermages go on believing that you're the stonefather," said Runnel. "I don't want to be Lord Runnel Stonefather."

"You have no choice," said Brickel. "Among stone-mages, that is your name, though we shorten it. 'Runnel Stanfar.'"

"But my common name, here on the streets of the city. Let me be...Runnel Cobbleskin. Your apprentice. Your servant. Let this skin be known as something that you did for me, to make me strong and tough."

"You really don't want to take your rightful place of authority?"

"I'm a child," said Runnel.

"You were man enough yesterday, to steal the lake from the wetwizards and burn it into steam." Brickel laughed. "Once I stopped being so terrified myself, it was really funny."

"If I had known what I was doing there at the bridge, I would never have done it," said Runnel.

"You should have obeyed me. But it turned out well."

"I'll obey you now," said Runnel.

Brickel laughed. "Except when you think I'm wrong."

The days and weeks and months passed by, and Runnel's new stoneskin did not stop him from growing taller, till he had a man's height. Stonemages came to the city, many of them to live there and take part in the government of the place, but many more merely to meet the young apprentice who had restored them to their holy city. Runnel went with them and stood in the circle when the leading rockbrothers built back the dome of living rock that had once enclosed the bodies of those who saved the city from the Verylludden.

They showed no outward sign of his prominence among them, lest the watermages realize that Runnel was their stonefather. But they all knew that it was Runnel whose power did most of the stoneshaping; that it was Runnel who drew up to the surface the fading outselves of the dead rockbrothers. He fashioned for them bodies of stone, which stood around the inside wall of the dome, their feet fused to the living rock. As long as their outselves persisted, they would have the use of these bodies; and when they faded, these would be their memorial.

When Runnel Cobbleskin was eighteen years old, by the nearest reckoning he could come up with, he went to Lark, who had long since come into her own as a birdfriend, keeping doves at the crest of Mitherjut that carried messages far and wide. He took her into his arms, and she held him close.

"Lark," said Runnel, "I want to hold you forever, the way the living stone holds the waters of the Mitherlough."

"I'm only a weak-skinned girl, and mostly water," she said. "You're too hardskinned for me now, Stanfar. How can I take a stone as my husband?"

"Gentle can be as good as soft," he answered. "And there's no burden I cannot lift for you."

"I have flown with my birds high above the earth," she said. "But I will make my nest with you." ◆